WHO LOVES
SAM GRANT?
by Delores Beckman

E. P. DUTTON   •   NEW YORK

Library of Congress Cataloging in Publication Data

Beckman, Delores.   Who loves Sam Grant?

Summary: Sophomore Samantha's life is complicated by
her on-and-off relationship with her school's handsome
quarterback, and by the bad-tempered parrot El Loro, a
rival school's stolen mascot, hidden in her garage.
[1. School stories] I. Title.
PZ7.B38174Wh 1983 [Fic] 82-18211
ISBN 0-525-44055-0

Published in the United States by E. P. Dutton, Inc.,
2 Park Avenue, New York, N.Y. 10016

Published simultaneously in Canada by Clarke,
Irwin & Company Limited, Toronto and Vancouver

Editor: Ann Durell   Designer: Claire Counihan

Printed in the U.S.A.   First Edition
10 9 8 7 6 5 4 3 2 1

Who Loves
Sam Grant?

ALSO BY DELORES BECKMAN

My Own Private Sky

to Jack, George and Ruth,
with special thanks to
Natasha Papousek

and for Maynard, of course

1

Sam Grant sat on one of the natural benches worn into the School Rock, her heart thumping as she stared down at her English book. Everything was visible from her vantage point—the student parking lot, the long row of windows on the far side of the quad, and, most important of all, the side door of the gymnasium. Students who habitually clustered around the Rock after the last bell had slowly drifted away. Sam held her breath. So far, so good.

Any minute now Bogie Benson would emerge from the gym, come loping across the quad, and stop at her feet. Sam would look up in an absent-minded way, push a wisp of hair out of her eyes, and exclaim, "Is football practice over already? Don't tell me I've missed the bus!"

"It's okay"—Bogie would smile in that heart-stopping way—"I'll give you a lift home."

And Sam would have the chance she had been waiting for since summer—a chance to win him back. The fact that he had dropped her for that new girl, Phyll Morton— the thought made Sam go hollow all over again—didn't mean it was written in stone. Sam could make Bogie see

1

what a mistake it had been, if only people would leave her alone with him for a little while.

Bogie's sudden appearance outside the gym sent Sam's thoughts into a tailspin. Breaking away from his team-mates in the horse-style gallop that had gained so many touchdowns for Treadwill High, he tucked one arm against his ribs and headed straight for the Rock. Sam's heart leaped. He was waving! She waved back, her book sliding to the grass as she jumped to her feet.

Then, without warning, Bogie swerved. He was not looking at her at all, but over her shoulder! From then on things seemed to be happening in slow motion. Bogie raised the tucked arm and threw an apple that soared in a looping arc and landed precisely at Phyll Morton's feet. Phyll scooped it up, her sun-bleached hair flying behind her, and ran with Bogie's hand locked in hers toward the parking lot.

Sam's eyes blurred. He hadn't even seen her. The humiliation of it brought a pain Sam had never felt before, even when Bogie had jilted her. For this time she had made a fool of herself, with Phyll Morton there to see. A new and puzzling despair overtook her.

What was happening? Why was she, Sam Grant, standing in the middle of the quad like some withering wall-flower? Boys weren't in the habit of falling over themselves in order to avoid her. Quite the opposite, in fact. Sam had always been one of the popular girls in school, never lacking for dates or invitations. Why was everything suddenly so *wrong*?

It was all Phyll Morton's fault. Before she came to town with her beach-blonde hair and California tan, Sam had been Bogie's girl—the steady girl of the hottest quarter-back in the Conference League. And before his, Pete Jamieson's. Pete might not be a football star, but he was one of the best-liked guys in school, as well as the nicest. It wasn't as if Sam had been sitting on the bench where boys were concerned.

Sam surveyed the empty quad, wanting to run and hide. Yet she had to find a ride home, and the best bet at this hour was her father, who always grubbed around in his math room until Maintenance swept him out. Heading for the row of classrooms and her locker, Sam wondered how she could face him—or anyone else—ever again.

The slow deliberate pace of someone coming around the corner was all too familiar. Oh, why did Murray Howell have to show up now, of all times? Sam hurried to her locker and began fumbling with the combination, hoping he wouldn't stop. But no, there he was, eyebrows raised in amused tolerance.

"Ahh, Samantha." He leaned against the lockers, flexing his long tanned fingers in their hand crutches. "How was Madrigals?"

"We're rehearsing at night now it's so close to festival time."

"Then why, pray tell, are you lolling about the hallowed halls at this late hour?"

"I was studying." Sam put her English book into the locker and dragged out several others.

"Study hall closed half an hour ago."

"Just a second while I write that down."

"The Plastic Look. Very becoming."

The whine of a motor hung in the air as Bogie's Ford spun out onto the street. Sam swallowed a lump in her throat and quipped, "Some day Bogie Benson is going to get suspended for speeding in the parking lot."

"Why, Samantha. Do I detect a note of scorn for dear old Bogie? It seems only yesterday he was at the top of your priority list."

3

Sam curbed the desire to throw a book at him. "I consider high school an opportunity to enrich my life with a variety of relationships."

"Bravo. You stole that line from your father, but bravo."

Sam headed for the classrooms. "Do you practice being obnoxious, Murray, or does it come with the elevated rank of senior?"

"I learned it all in the back room at TG&Y."

"Excuse me. I have to find my father for a ride home."

"Your father is in a faculty meeting of some importance. I was there for the *Echoes* and left when it became—"

"Blast. Now I'll have to call Mother."

Murray followed her out the main entrance, the late afternoon sun catching his unruly blond hair. The tanned face with its high forehead and blue eyes was a perfect setting for his wide mocking smile. Nothing, not even the fact that he was crippled, seemed to detract from his perpetual calm. To Sam, the braces on his legs were a part of him, just as the crutches were an extension of his arms.

Sam had forgotten the name of the town where Murray had lived before moving next door to them—she'd been four and he almost seven when they'd become neighbors—but it was a town that had made the papers. Doctors there had used a perfectly good batch of vaccine on hundreds of children, only to have one of them come down with polio. The fact that Murray had been that one child was something he seemd to have forgotten, too. He was simply Murray-next-door, and the bane of Sam's life.

As they made their way to the telephone booth on the corner, Sam put Murray out of her mind. She had made a fool of herself on the Rock, but that didn't mean there was no tomorrow. The Backwards Dance was still weeks away. There would be chances to get Bogie Benson back

4

before then. All she had to do was find some way to get him unglued from Phyll Morton for a while.

"What lucky swain are you inviting to the Backwards Dance?" Murray asked.

"I'm tossing some names into a hat." Did he read minds? Even her best friend Heather Grayson hadn't asked her *that* yet. "Actually I haven't given much thought to the Backwards Dance."

"Which is Samantha's way of saying she has thought of little else."

Sam turned on him. "Go stick your needles into someone else, Murray! Some helpless little kid, or a stray cat, maybe."

"Tut, tut, Samantha."

"And tell me. Why do you persist in calling me Samantha when everyone in the whole school calls me Sam?"

"Because it's your name."

"And another thing! Just because we have lived next door to each other almost all of our lives and you are practically family doesn't give you the right to keep tabs on me and pry into my affairs. Who do you think you are? My keeper?"

Murray's smile took wings.

Sam was all but shouting now. "I haven't done a thing in simply eons that you haven't been standing around with that superior smile, handing down messages from your own private tower of wisdom. You have supervised my school schedules, study habits, ability to play the clarinet, and selection of clothes. Now you seem determined to set yourself up as chief counselor in the romance department. Once and for all, Murray, I am perfectly capable of taking care of myself."

Sam slammed the door of the phone booth and rummaged in her bag for a coin.

Murray pushed at the door and handed her a dime. "Dial T for temper."

Sam dropped the dime, picked it up, deposited it, and dialed, only to hear the busy signal. She leaned against the shelf in utter frustration while Murray tapped on the window with a maddening staccato. "Who do you think will win Friday's game?"

Sam turned her back. If he thought he was going to get an answer out of her he was very much mistaken.

"Ah, well—it matters little, really," he went on. "It's the one with Fairview that counts. We can win them all and still lose the big game."

Murray said *big game* as if it were some kind of child's play instead of the most important event of the whole school year. As if they played Fairview every week. As if Fairview and Treadwill hadn't been arch rivals for years and years. In spite of herself, Sam heard herself saying through the glass, "We'll win the big one."

Without waiting for an answer, Sam dialed again. This time the phone rang endlessly on the other end while Murray continued his relentless tapping. It was no use. Her mother must have gone outside. Everything had gone wrong since Sam had perched herself on the edge of the School Rock, and it wasn't going to change now. As if to prove it, Pete Jamieson pulled over to the curb in an ancient van and stopped.

Of all people to come along, it would have to be Pete. Sam had never felt comfortable around him since dropping him for Bogie Benson. She gathered her books and opened the booth with what she hoped was a friendly smile. "Hi, Pete."

He leaned out, his red hair catching the sun. "You guys want a ride?"

There was nothing to do but climb onto the high seat,

6

with Murray squeezing in beside her until there was scarcely room for her books. Pete was always working on one antique car or another, but this was a new one to Sam. "What am I riding in?" she asked.

"You and I, my dear Samantha," Murray said, "are the first passengers in this completely restored 1911 Model Delivery Car, fully equipped with brass windshield, three oil lamps, speedometer, horn and tools. *And,* genuine wire-spoked wheels!"

Pete grinned, pushing something with his feet while he fiddled with a lever on the steering wheel.

"It's—very nice," Sam told him.

"Magnificent," Murray said. "It sounds great."

It sounded to Sam as if it would never get to her street, let alone her house, but it did in its own poky, purring way. Once stopped, it continued to vibrate smoothly in every core.

Sam couldn't ever remember feeling so depressed.

2

Murray, still talking about United terminals and Kingston carburetors, finally eased his crutches to the curb in front of Sam's house. Pete had been listening, while stealing glances at Sam. Now he asked, "Would you like to go for a little ride, Sam? Get a Coke or something?"

Climbing down with her books made not looking at his

earnest face easier. "Thanks, Pete, but I have to study."

She was almost to the front steps when her mother came around from the side yard exclaiming about the van. "It looks great, Peter. You must have worked awfully hard on it."

"Thanks, Mrs. Grant. I'm a hunchback at sixteen."

Pete's easy way with people, combined with her mother's quick laugh, caused Sam to feel a twinge of regret. "Some other time, Pete? It really is a neat car."

"Tomorrow, maybe?"

"Oh, dear. Tomorrow's my clarinet lesson."

"Sure. Plenty of time." Pete pushed hair out of his eyes. "Well, I'd better be going."

Sam wondered why she had ever thought Pete Jamieson was so exciting. She had practically gone steady with him until Bogie had come along, and compared to Bogie, Pete was pass the potatoes. A nice boy, but pass the potatoes. She gave a long sigh and started up the steps. *Bogie.* At last she could go up to her room and lie on the bed and think. She could plan a way to get him back if only everyone would stop crowding in on her. If only people would leave her alone.

"Will you take the trimmings to the alley for me, Sam?"

"Mother, I really do have to study."

Her mother had already turned back to Murray. "So you're doing a biology paper for Mr. Hampshire. What on?"

"The mating habits of the South American tree toad."

Their voices followed Sam all the way to the alley, where she dumped the plastic bag into the trash barrel. If they kept on talking about tree toads and the Beanstalk (which was what everyone in school called the incredibly tall and skinny Mr. Hampshire), she might get away after all. But she had no more than entered the backyard again when she saw her father coming in the front.

"Did I hear Hampshire's name? Genius, no doubt about it. If you can get past the—"

"Tree toads," her mother giggled.

Sam's father crossed the yard carrying his briefcase and the usual assortment of books and papers, leaned to kiss her mother, and called, "Hi, Murray. Hi, Sammie, baby."

"Daddy, *please*. How can someone who is a sophomore in high school be a baby?"

"Sorry, baby." He deposited his briefcase on a lawn chair and ran a hand through his graying hair. "Big flap on campus when I left, as Murray knows. The principal of Fairview called and said El Loro was missing."

"Oh, that awful parrot," Sam sniffed. "Who'd care?"

"He's their school mascot," Murray reminded her. "And the big game's not too far away now."

"There is more than a hint of suspicion as to who took the poor creature," Sam's father said.

"Some of our jocks at Treadwill," Murray surmised.

Sam wrinkled her forehead. "Why do they call him El Loro?"

"It's *parrot* in Spanish. And it's tradition to steal mascots at big game time. Remember when they stole our goat, Godfrey, last year?"

"There's going to be trouble," Sam's father said, looking suddenly tired. "The administration of both schools is getting weary of these childish pranks. If you're right and some of our players did take that bird, they'd better think twice about keeping it. There's too much bad blood between the two schools as it is, according to Mr. Coopersmith."

Sam pricked up her ears. There had been some sort of

9

hassle last year when Fairview made off with Godfrey. What had they done to the boys who had stolen him? She hadn't been all that interested in football then, not having started going steady with Bogie yet. Music had always been her thing. Sam pitied whoever had stolen El Loro, though. If rumors were correct, more than one person had regretted poking a finger too near his cage.

But who cared about a silly parrot? If only they would all stop talking about it, Murray would go home and she could escape. "Excuse me," she said, "I'm thirsty."

"Good," her father said, "I could use a Pensa Cola myself."

Sam's mother laughed. "Just the thing to make you forget the trouble at the old Treadmill."

Murray winked. "I'll help with the Pensa Cola, Samantha."

Sam groaned.

Sam stretched facedown on her bed. Now that she finally had some time to think, she couldn't bear her thoughts. Watching Bogie grab Phyll's hand and run. Putting up with Murray and his superior jibes. That awful ride home in Pete's precious van. The interminable talk about tree toads, the Beanstalk, and the disappearance of Fairview's parrot.

Sam rolled over and dialed Heather Grayson's number. Heather always listened, even if she was a bit blunt at times. Sam didn't care. If she didn't talk to someone, they would have to peel her off the woodwork. Besides, what were best friends for?

"Hello." Heather made the sucking sound that meant she was biting what was left of her fingernails.

"It's Sam. What took you so long to answer?"

"I was studying. I am going to get a D on Eaglethorpe's *Julius Caesar* exam. Say something to cheer me."

"My father just invited Murray in for a Pensa Cola."

Heather laughed her horse laugh. "Do they really make that stuff in Pepsi Cola, Florida?"

"You're as bad as my mother. If people would stop laughing at my father's dreadful puns, maybe he'd—"

"Do you remember the time Pete's Yamaha broke down in front of your house and your father came out and asked him what was wrong with the old—the old Omaha?"

"Heather, listen! Daddy just came home and said that the mascot from Fairview has been—"

"—stolen."

"How'd *you* know?"

"Murray asked me to help on a student committee, but it conflicted with Marching Band. How'd *you* do out on the Rock trying to waylay Bogie Benson?"

Sam envied Heather psyching people out that way. If she could psych people out that way, maybe she would know why Bogie had thrown her over for Phyll Morton. "Not so hot."

"An honest confession is good for the soul. Continue."

Sam blinked back tears. "Oh, Heather, why does Phyll Morton have to have everything?"

"I didn't know she did."

"All those great California clothes! Looking like she

11

lived on the beach all her life. Acting so sophisticated."

"If you call smoking in the girls' room sophisticated."

"I wish I knew how Bogie really feels about her."

"Tom Hanson says he's down for the count."

"So Tom Hanson's the town crier now, is that it?"

"He also says Bogie's going to get cut from the team if his grades don't pick up. And don't tell me he's too busy with football practice and training. More like busy tearing around on those balloon tires with a steering wheel attached, drinking beer and dancing all hours at the Crumbler."

"You don't know if that's true! People are just jealous of Bogie because he's so big on the team and—"

Heather sighed the way she did when she had run out of fingernails. "Bull. You're the one who's jealous—of Phyll."

"Ha! A girl who steals other girls' boyfriends?"

"She didn't steal Bogie. He lay down and let her run over him like a Mack truck."

Heather's advice had suddenly lost its appeal. "What guy are you asking to the Backwards Dance?"

"I'll tell you only if you promise not to tell my mother. My mother has always been scared to death no guy would ask me to a dance, and now she's scared no guy will go if *I* ask him."

Sam juggled the phone. Heather's mother came from one of the oldest families in town and was so beautiful she made people's eyes water. She'd had three husbands after Heather's father and was now Through With Men For Life. "I won't tell. Who?"

"Jerry Petersen."

"Not Tom?" Sam was startled.

"Tom's a senior. He's too old for me."

Sam knew how much better Heather liked Tom Hanson, and how awkward and twitchy Jerry Petersen was. "That's neat. You and Jerry have a lot in common—Marching Band—and—"

"—being six feet tall. At least when I'm dancing with him I won't have to look down on his cowlick."

As you would with Tom, Sam thought. She had to admit that Heather had a real problem; it had started in eighth grade. She was so tall she played right alongside Jerry in the Marching Band, even though she had to wear foam rubber pads on her legs to keep the snares from beating her black and blue.

"Who are you asking?" Heather wanted to know.

"I haven't made up my mind."

"Tell the truth. You're waiting for lightning to strike Phyll Morton so you can ask Bogie."

The misery of the whole day bunched itself behind Sam's eyelids. "I'll tell the truth! I am sick and tired of hearing you say 'Tell the truth'!" Her eyes went cloudy as she slammed the phone into its cradle. "I hate her. I hate her!" Burying her face in the pillow, she cried, sniffled, and cried some more.

4

Sam didn't want to go to school the next morning. There were too many people to face. Heather, Murray, Bogie. Bogie and Phyll, together, always together. But there was that English exam, and she had to practice with the Pep

13

Band for Friday's rally. Besides, a Grant never stayed home from school unless it was contagious.

She went downstairs. Her father had gone to school early and her mother was standing by the sink looking out the window. The only sound was the hum of the washing machine from the utility room. "Good morning."

Her mother jumped. "Oh, Sam. I didn't hear you come down."

Sam dished some cereal and poured a glass of juice. After a few swallows, she picked up her books. "I'd better run."

"But you haven't finished your breakfast."

"I'm not hungry."

"Sam—if there's anything you—"

"I'm going to be late, Mother." And in the next breath, "The washing machine's running over."

Her mother pulled the plug, grabbed a broom and began sweeping water out the back door. "Run along. It's not the end of the world."

Sam walked to the bus thinking how glad she was her father hadn't been there when the washing maching went haywire. It would have been the last straw. "Always knew something would happen to the old RCA Squirrel Pool sooner or later," he would have corned.

What would it be like to have normal parents? A mother who cried and screamed and demanded to know why her daughter's eyes were red and swollen at the dinner table? Who swore when things went wrong, like Heather's mother? Or a father who was casually elegant, like Phyll's father with his cashmere sports jackets and Gucci shoes?

Sam saw Murray waiting at the bus stop and was barely able to match his brilliant smile. "How did you get to be so sweet and all forgiving, Murray?"

14

"I did it in six days and rested on the seventh."

They got on the bus together. Heather climbed on at her corner and sat down directly behind the driver without looking around. Sam inhaled a fierce breath and went to sit beside her. "I'm sorry I was such a pig."

"No problem. We all lose our cool at times." Heather opened her *Julius Caesar* and began studying.

Sam knew Murray was watching but wouldn't give him the satisfaction of looking his way. As she stared out the window, Bogie went roaring by in his Ford, with Phyll snuggled beside him, a fur hat topping her honey-striped hair. Sam watched until all that was visible was undercarriage, and two outsized tires. A lump settled into the pit of her stomach.

When the bus stopped at school, Sam stumbled down the steps with a muttered "See you" to Heather and Murray. Fumbling with the combination to her locker, she automatically glanced past the corner and down seven metal doors, top tier. Her heart skipped rope and stood still. How did Bogie manage to stand out that way, as if someone had drawn a circle around him? Or had she programmed herself to pick out his shag of brown hair even in a crowd of milling students?

Sam pulled herself together and jammed books into her locker. If Bogie caught her looking at him like a sick swan he would smile that uneasy smile, and Sam didn't think she could take that today. Yesterday, maybe. Yesterday she might even have taken it as an excuse to make her way over to him with a smile of her own. But that was before that agonizing scene at the Rock, and Heather telling her Bogie was down for the count over Phyll. That was yesterday, when things had seemed worth fighting for.

Sam walked hurriedly down the corridor, unaware of

the babble around her. When exactly had she stopped hoping for a chance to *talk* to Bogie and settled for a chance just to *see* him? Was that part of the recovery process? Sam didn't know. Her heart had never been broken before. Would it help to call Crisis Hot Line? "Hello," she could say, "You don't know me, but I am fifteen years old and this boy used to like me very much but he doesn't anymore and I feel so bad I want to die. Can you help me please?"

The squawker blared a call for special assembly, and it was only then that Sam realized something unusual was happening. She felt a persistent tugging at her sleeve. "Hey," Heather was saying, "assembly's right—you're going left." She peered into Sam's eyes. "Amnesia. I wish I'd thought of that on Eaglethorpe's exam day! I was going to settle down with my wrists and a razor."

Sam had to laugh, and suddenly the whole scene came into focus, raucous and high-pitched. Students were moving towards the auditorium on small waves of excitement and curiosity. Sam heard the words *El Loro* and *Fairview* over and over. There was a bottleneck at both sets of doors. Heather said, "I feel a tackle coming on," and parted the sea of students in a forward drive, dragging Sam with her.

Through the crush Sam saw the usual clique of senior wheels slouching in the back row. Bogie was with them, feet propped carelessly onto the seat in front of him. No other junior would have dared invade the senior quorum. But then no other junior was a star quarterback who looked as if he belonged there.

Finding herself front row center, Sam muttered, "Why don't we go up and sit on the stage where we can *really* be conspicuous?"

"I like to sit where they can see me," Heather said. "Counter-resistance to my mother's constant urge to hide me in a closet."

"You're making that up." Sam watched the stage. Pete Jamieson was one of two boys setting up mikes. He kept looking at her out of the corner of his eye. Why was it that the boys a girl wanted to look at her never looked, while the ones she didn't always did? She smiled at Pete. He caught his foot in a length of cord, righted himself, and smiled back.

Murray sat down beside her. "Ahh, Mr. Coopersmith himself. Flanked by an inordinate contingent of brass. I should have brought my camera."

Sam watched as the principal took a stand behind the mike, surrounded by the guidance counselor, head coach, and assistant coach. He tapped the mike for attention, gave up, and cleared his throat in an effort to be heard above the din. "Good morning, ladies and gentlemen." The whistles in the back gradually subsided. "This won't take long."

"Take all day," Heather mumbled. "I can sharpen my razor later."

"I have called this special assembly to tell you that Fairview High's mascot, a parrot named El Loro, has been—is missing." He waited out more whistles and laughter. "Since this concerns the sports area more than Administration, I have asked Coach Gilmore to speak to you."

"This is no laughing matter," the coach said, "so knock it off. While a certain amount of horsing around can be expected in the heat of a close football season, there are limits. I am not going to hassle you with suppositions or accusations. I am only going to tell you—"

"—leaving out the ifs, ands, and buts," Murray recited.

"—leaving out the ifs, ands, and buts, that the mascot of Fairview is gone. He is a rare and delicate bird."

His words were drowned in a chorus of catcalls. "He's going for the ramrod approach," Murray said. "Can't lose control."

The coach lowered his voice to a menacing growl. "Now you people listen. I am not saying that anyone from Treadwill took that parrot. But I am saying that if someone did, then there'd better be some serious second thoughts on the matter." He flexed his wrist and stared stonily at his watch. "Shall we say in the next twenty-four hours?" Stepping aside, he braced himself as if for a forward tackle.

Mr. Coopersmith moved to the mike, pushing at his glasses. "That about covers it. Treadwill High cannot be responsible should anything happen to Fairview's mascot because of a careless prank. There is considerable pressure from their administration for the parrot to be returned safely at once. In case anyone is harboring the idea that this is not a serious matter, I can only say that if the parrot is not returned within the allotted time, more stringent measures will have to be taken, which could include expelling the guilty parties. Assembly is dismissed. Please go to your classes."

Heather seemed reluctant to leave. "What do you think, Murray?"

"I think that someone is sweating out a pretty iffy situation. Along with wondering what to feed a rare species of parrot named El Loro."

Sam picked up her books. "I'm just glad it isn't me."

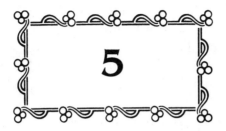

5

The *Julius Caesar* exam was a breeze. Sam was finished fifteen minutes before anyone else. She sat alternately staring out the window and watching Heather bite what was left of her fingernails. Exam fever filled the stuffy room, running at epidemic level.

Pete Jamieson squirmed, sucking the end of his pencil. Other students frowned, stared at the ceiling, and shuffled their feet. "Ten minutes." Miss Eaglethorpe stared at her watch as if it might start bonging out the seconds. For lack of anything else to do, Sam took out her notebook and wrote in bold letters: WHO STOLE EL LORO?

She quickly eliminated a girl, or girls, even in this liberated era. The same went for the team. The logistics of getting the whole team involved in such a caper were mind boggling. More than likely two or three boys. But which two or three? Stealing El Loro was no small task. It was rumored his cage hung right in the Fairview locker room. Sam wrote: TWO BOYS WITH VERVE AND LUCK.

Feeling a ripple across her neck, Sam looked up to see the cool gray eyes of Miss Eaglethorpe perusing the notebook over her shoulder. To Sam's utter amazement, one of the lids closed in a slow, deliberate wink. "Nice work, Samantha."

The *Echoes* hit the corridors during the last period of the day, and as usual on Wednesdays, students gathered in knots to digest the news. A headline leaped out at Sam as she walked to the lockers with Heather: EL LORO MISSING. "Why didn't Murray come right out and say he was kidnapped?"

"Because he can't prove that he was. A good editor sticks to the facts, ma'am. Listen: 'It is hoped that students will treat this matter with the seriousness it deserves, and that the Case of the Missing Parrot will soon be resolved.' "

Reading some student interviews, Sam's heart began a curious racing. "Listen to what Bogie says. 'What's to go ape about? Once the big game is over, El Loro will show up safe and sound.' "

And then Bogie himself was leaning over her shoulder for a closer look. "What do you know? Murray's snoops got something right for a change."

Sam wanted to say something, do something, that would set his wheels spinning, but with one of his hands casually draped around her neck and a lock of his shaggy brown hair all but brushing her cheek, she found it impossible to breathe. "Do—do you really think he'll be all right? El Loro, I mean?"

Bogie sucked a cut on his index finger. "What's to worry? Parrots are tough birds. A little feed and water—"

"And make sure his cage is covered at night. My mother had a cockatoo once, and—" Sam's chest thumped in desperation. Here was her one big chance with Bogie and she was mumbling about the care and feeding of parrots! She gave her head a toss and smiled into his iced-tea eyes.

20

"Isn't it crazy what some kids will do to rev things up for the big game, Bogie?"

"Yeah, sure."

"Who do you think stole him? I mean—you're on the team—"

Bogie shook hair out of his eyes. "Anyone smart enough to get that bird out of a locker room isn't going to give himself away." He glanced at his watch. "Gotta split. Late for practice."

He was gone. Sam couldn't even see his gorgeous back once he had turned the corner. Her hands felt hollow as she opened her locker, her head light and fuzzy. If only she'd had the sense to say something clever—make him notice her the way she'd always been able to do before Phyll Morton came along.

"What a male chauvinist pig," Heather said.

"I'll be late for Orchestra," Sam told her, and left.

She was out of breath when seated in the music room. Being with Bogie for such a short time made everything twice as unbearable. There *had* to be a way to get him back. She would do anything. Anything. Mr. De Browne had not arrived yet, so Sam laid her clarinet across her knees and dug the *Echoes* out of her bag. On the last page was one of Murray's popular cartoons. A bedraggled parrot drooped in a cage, and underneath, a caption said: If they keep this up I'm gonna start talking.

Hearing a rap on the music stand, Sam raised her clarinet. Halfway through the piece, her eyes met Murray's over his flute. He played steadily, eyes shining as if someone had lit a candle behind them. Sam smiled, which was difficult to do while playing a clarinet. Was this how football players felt when they huddled together on a field? Did Bogie feel this surge of excitement when he'd

21

made a spectacular throw? Her heart soared. He *had* stopped at her locker. He *could* have gone on. And there had been something about his *smile* . . .

Would she ever know how Bogie felt? And he? Would he understand how *she* felt, playing so well, with all the other musicians playing with her until the whole room seemed to swell?

It was only when the piece was ended that Sam saw her father in the doorway. With a nod to Mr. De Browne, he motioned for her to step outside. "A call from Santa Barbara," he said, taking her hand. "Grandmother Harrington's had a heart attack. Your mother's going out there right away—we have to get home."

Sam put her clarinet away, suddenly shaky, and for some reason turned at the door to look at Murray. Caught unaware, his face was anxious. Then he flashed his brilliant smile.

Sam had never seen her mother in such a state. While she seemed to move with her usual efficiency, there was a kind of numbed frenzy in her voice. "I've made a list," she said, waving a piece of paper. "And no TV dinners, promise."

"I don't mind TV dinners in an emergency," Sam's father said. "Besides—we can eat in the school cafeteria."

"They serve dog food in the school cafeteria."

"I never said that. Must have been Sam."

Sam couldn't believe her ears. Here they were, worried half-sick over Grandmother Harrington, talking about food. Next thing, her mother would be telling her what to eat for breakfast.

"And eat a good breakfast." Sam's mother took a sweater from the drawer, rolled it, unrolled it, and put it back in the drawer. "She's never had a sick day in her life."

Sam's father retrieved the sweater, stuffed it into the suitcase and snapped it shut. Guiding her mother out to the car, he turned to Sam. "Good girl. You've got the flight bag."

Sam felt her mother's arms around her. "When will you be back?"

"I don't know. I'll just have to wait and see how—how things are when I get there." She pulled Sam close. "Heavens. How are you going to get to Madrigal practice?"

Sam scrambled for an answer. "I'll call Lucy Adams. She has her license now."

Her father's jaw opened, then shut. "Come straight home, you hear?"

"And eat something," her mother called. "There's left-over—"

"Don't worry." Sam waved until the car turned the corner, then went inside. The house seemed strangely quiet. She turned on the fluorescent lights in the kitchen even though it wasn't dark yet, and called Lucy Adams.

"Sure," the answer came. "I have a full tank of gas and my parents are gone for the evening. Fun and games."

It made Sam nervous. "Listen, Lucy—I have to get home early."

"Let's try and keep that in mind," Lucy said, and hung up.

Sam opened the refrigerator and took out an apple and a glass of nonfat milk. Lucy Adams was something else, all sweetness and light on the outside and a hellcat on the inside. Carrying the apple and milk, she went up to her room and dialed Heather's number.

"Hello. Oh—Sam. Where'd you disappear to after Orchestra? I looked all over for you. Did your father tell you that—?"

"My father didn't have time to tell me anything. My grandmother's had a heart attack and he's taking Mother to the airport."

"Oh, I'm really sorry, Sam." Heather paused. "Seems unimportant now, but—your father has been appointed faculty adviser for Treadwill on the El Loro caper."

"Good. If anyone can get to the bottom of things, Daddy can. Listen, Heather, I have to run. Lucy Adams's picking me up for Madrigal practice. It was just—I mean, the house was so empty—and—"

"Sure."

"Call you tomorrow. Bye."

The house became increasingly lonely once the sun went down. Leaving lights on in both the living room and kitchen, Sam locked the front door and went to wait for Lucy in the porch swing. Murray was standing at the bottom of the step. "I'm sorry about your grandmother."

"Thanks. Mother is pretty upset."

He lowered himself into the swing beside her, pushing with a crutch to set them moving. "Practice as usual?"

"Lucy Adams is picking me up."

"Be sure and fasten your seat belt."

"We learned a lot in kindergarten today, Murray. In Show and Tell, I fastened my seat belt on the very first try."

"You always were a smart girl." Murray stopped the swing. "Here's your little Hell's Angel."

Lucy whizzed a black car with orange stripes to a stop, tires scraping on the curb. "Hi, Murray. How do you like my new wheels?"

"Much better than your peripheral vision."

"It's got everything. Power windows, tape deck, leather seats—all the extra extras."

"But no roll bars."

"He's funny," Lucy said as they barreled away. "Don't you think Murray's *funny*, Sam?"

"Not as funny as you'll be when you get a ticket for going fifty in a twenty-five miles an hour zone."

Lucy's laugh tinkled. "My father can fix tickets. He knows everyone at city hall."

"But can he fix *me* when I'm wrapped around a telephone pole?" Sam closed her eyes as they went around a corner on the wrong side of the street, forcing her mind into blankness. Either they would get there alive or they wouldn't. Worrying was as useless as thinking, and thinking was strictly a pain these days. No matter how much Sam thought, she always came back where she started.

Everything was all mixed up, and she was the most mixed up of all.

7

Sam stood on the steps of the music building and watched Lucy's Trans Am move toward her. Instead of stopping to pick her up, it spun blithely past, two people snuggled into the seat belts. Sam had seen Matt Masterson hanging around during Madrigal practice and now she knew why. Lucy Adams had deserted her for a pickup.

Sam spent a minute being angrier than she could ever remember, and another one telling herself it was all a joke and Lucy would surely come back. By then it was nine fifteen, the campus was thoroughly deserted, and Sam was thoroughly scared.

She had never been alone at school in the dark. Even with the night lights, everything looked twice as big as in the daytime. The familiar lines of the round library building looked magnified against the wind-driven clouds, like some giant silo filled with owls and bats.

When a piece of shrubbery brushed against her arm, Sam jumped quickly onto the grass. She had to think. Was her father home from the airport yet? Rummaging in her purse, she found a lone dime. Enough to call him, and if her father wasn't there, a taxi. But how could she pay the taxi fare if her father wasn't home when she got there?

"Help!" she said aloud, and could hear her father saying,

"Don't just stand there. *Do something.*" Sam inhaled a fierce breath and struck out across the quad. It was darker out there, but faster, and she forced herself to walk because running would only make things scarier than they already were.

"Let's pretend," she whispered, calling on an old childhood shelter when frightened. "It's a game of Hide and Seek. Everyone is here, they're just hiding. All I have to do is find them." It was no use and never had been. When Sam was hiding, someone always found her, and when she was seeking, she never found anyone.

Good. There was the School Rock. She was halfway across the quad.

"AAARRRRHHHHHHKKKKKK!" The bloodcurdling squawk shattered the air, turning Sam's legs to mush.

"AAARRRRHHHHHHKKKKKK!" It came again, this time accompanied by a rustle of feathers. Sam peered at something moving on the Rock and found herself face to face with the parrot, El Loro.

Thoughts whizzed through her brain like tapes in Fast Forward. What was he doing out *here?* Maybe he hadn't been stolen after all. Maybe he'd somehow gotten away from Fairview! But Fairview was *miles* from here. No. Someone had had to bring him. And if he was as rare and delicate a bird as everyone had said, wouldn't he die of exposure if she left him here?

Sam leaned closer. He didn't look delicate. He looked as if he could take care of himself and then some. But she couldn't leave him out there, it would be inhumane. "Nice birdie, nice birdie," she cooed, reaching a tentative hand.

His beak flew down, barely missing her finger. "Fairview's the best, the best, the best! Murder the rest, the rest, the rest!"

27

Pulling back, Sam croaked, "Polly want a cracker?"

"He doesn't want a cracker," a voice said from the other side of the Rock. "He wants an arm or a leg."

"Is—is that you, Bogie?"

"Yeah, it's me." He stepped out from behind the Rock, nursing a cut finger. "Hi, Sammie."

Sam went limp with relief. If she had to be out in the middle of the quad at night with an evil-tempered parrot, she was glad Bogie Benson was there with her. "Wh-what are *you* doing here?"

"Chasing this miserable bag of bones and feathers." He moved closer. "What *you're* doing here is a better question."

"I was stranded after Madrigal practice. By Lucy Adams."

"It figures. She's probably dancing her little feet off at the Crumbler."

It didn't matter. Bogie was here. Bogie would see that everything was under control. "What's that?"

He was pulling a large cardboard box with some kind of sliding screen from behind the Rock. "I'm going to put him in this. I tried baiting him with a piece of apple, but the devil prefers human flesh. In the hassle, he got away from me."

"From where?"

"The ticket office under the bleachers. It was only a temporary hiding place. Seth—I mean, this other boy— was supposed to take him home and keep him in his garage, but he chickened out on me, the chicken."

So it was Bogie and Seth Harper who had stolen El Loro! "But what will you do with him?"

"You mean before or after I wrassle him into this box?"

El Loro had hunched himself into one huge malevolent

28

ball of feathers. "Maybe I could get his attention long enough for you to clamp the box over him." It was Sam's chance to make an impression on Bogie. "You could pretend you're leaving. Take the box with you, and I'll talk to him."

Bogie made circles in the air around his head. "Nobody can talk to that buzzard."

"I can try." When he didn't answer, Sam said, "Don't just stand there. *Do something.*"

Bogie shrugged. "Bye." He waved and slouched off into the shadows, dragging the box with him.

Raising her voice in an imitation of El Loro's squawk, Sam yelled, "Treadwill can, can, can! Treadwill will, will, will!"

El Loro shrieked as if mortally wounded. "Fairview's the best, the best, the best! Murder the rest, the rest, the rest!"

Down came the box from behind. There was a horrendous beating of wings from the inside as Sam rushed to help Bogie hold it tight. "N-now what?"

"Hold this screen. When I inch the box over, slide it under."

Sam bit her lip. "Where's the notch? Oh, there. I can feel it." She edged the screen into the groove, very much aware of El Loro's frantic squawkings. Inch by inch, the screen slid under the box until Bogie was holding the box free. El Loro let loose another torrent of abuse. "Murder the rest, the rest, the rest!"

Sam held a hand over her thumping chest. "What next?"

"Just a cage to hold this monster and a place to hide him until after the big game, that's all." Bogie looked at Sam with a grateful smile. "You've been really super, Sammie. You want a ride home?"

29

Sam's stomach rolled over. "I—I don't know if I want to ride with *him* or not."

"He'll be okay for a while. If only I had a place to hide him." Bogie was looking at her as if she were his best girl again. "Maybe you can help me think of something on the way?"

Sam swallowed, opened her mouth, shut it, and opened it again. "I—my mother—I mean, there's this cage. She had a cockatoo once—she inherited it when my Aunt Tisha died. The cage is in the—the studio over our—our garage."

"You've got a studio over your garage?"

"No one uses it except for storage."

Bogie lifted the box. "Something tells me you've found yourself a home, you buzzard."

"Oh, no! I couldn't, Bogie—"

"Just for tonight? I'll come and get him tomorrow, I promise."

"But—if my father found out— No, I'm sorry, Bogie, I just can't."

The silence seemed endless, then Bogie began walking away. "It's okay. No sweat."

Sam watched him go, the box held clumsily under one arm. What would he do with El Loro? And how was she going to get home? Sam tried to tell herself she still had the telephone booth and the dime, but something was propelling her forward. "Bogie?"

He whirled around.

"I—I guess it'll be all right. Just for tonight."

He ran back and kissed her. "I knew you wouldn't let me down, Sammie Lou. Thanks."

They walked the quad with the box between them. Sam felt as if someone had drained the blood from her veins and pumped them full of air. Bogie Benson had called her Sammie Lou, something that had always been special just between them. She sighed. *Sammie Lou.*

As they reached the car, El Loro yelled, "Murder the rest, the rest, the rest!"

8

"Has anyone ever told you you're an angel?"

Sam felt weak. Was Bogie Benson actually standing in their old garage studio? Could that truly be Fairview's missing parrot in her mother's discarded cockatoo cage? How could her hands be hot while her tongue was frozen? Her neck swiveled between Bogie and the window with clocklike regularity and wouldn't stop. It was insane. Either her father's lights would beam in the dark below or they wouldn't.

"You saved my life," Bogie said.

Sam didn't want to save his life. She wanted him to leave and take El Loro with him before her father came home. How could she account for being up in the garage studio with a boy, let alone being a partner in the case of the missing parrot? There went her neck again. "I—I think we'd better go."

"Sure." Bogie turned a pocket inside out, dumping bird-

31

seed onto a table. "Just feed him before and after school and he'll be okay."

Sam draped an old tablecloth over the cage. "At least he's not making that fearful racket anymore."

"Are you cold? Get your coat. Are you cold? Get your coat."

Bogie stared at the parrot. "He's bananas."

Sam turned off the lights and the darkness brought an almost dizzying relief. She clung to the railing as they went down the stairs. They were safe! Her father hadn't come home and caught them. Bogie's fingers closed tightly over her own. "You are one great girl, Sammie Lou."

Sam thought she might faint. Her father would come home and find her collapsed on the lawn. Now if she could only relax. Look at Bogie without sap running out of her ears. Stop jumping around like a jack-in-the-box every time a car turned the corner.

Was he going to kiss her? The moon scooted around a cloud, instant silver. The air was filled with sounds she had never heard before, a fugue in two different keys. Even the leaves fluttering to the ground were keeping time, and Sam was a part of it all. She held her breath while the moon dipped behind a cloud and Bogie bent his mouth towards hers.

The telephone rang.

"Excuse me," Sam gasped.

"I'd better split," Bogie said.

Turning for a second at the door, Sam saw his familiar back, shoulders hunched, hands jammed deep into pockets. The sound of his whistling joined the roar of the souped-up motor and the clamorous jangle of the telephone. "Hello," she panted, only to hear a click at the other end. Had it been her father? Her mother? Was her grandmother worse? Was she—

Sam wouldn't let herself think, not about anything. She would stand very still and take ten deep breaths. How quiet the house was. As if no one were ever coming home again.

The telephone shrieked, and Sam grabbed it. "Hello!"

Heather's flat voice righted the world. "I got to thinking—it must be awfully lonely in that empty house— Why don't—"

"Heather, listen. If I tell you something, you've got to promise not to tell a living soul."

"Croth my heart. Honeth and thruly."

"This is serious, Heather."

"Look, Sam. I have been keeping secrets ever since I promised my mother I wouldn't tell her second husband that she'd had five gin and tonics and missed most of the Easter program in kindergarten where I was being a real live bunny."

"Okay." Sam took a ragged breath. "El Loro is out in our garage studio."

"*Who* is out *where?*"

Sam froze. "I have to hang up. No. Yes. I'll call you later."

Sam was standing in the hall in time to see her father come through the door. "Oh, Daddy! I'm so glad you're home!"

"What a night." He smiled wearily, shedding his coat. "You'll never believe it."

Sam took his coat. "Come out to the kitchen and I'll make some coffee. You can tell me all about it." What sheer unadulterated bliss—hearing about someone *else's* miserable night.

After he had gone to bed, Sam tried to sleep, but her mind was like a beehive. She *had* to tell Heather the rest of the story or go crazy. She felt a momentary pang as she dialed because it was so late—but what were best friends for?

All Heather said was, "I've been waiting for you to call. Begin at the beginning."

Sam told her everything, accompanied by the continuous sound of nails being chewed to the quick.

9

Sam woke the next morning to see her father standing by her bed. "Hey—you're all ready for school."

"Astute observation. You will also observe as you go downstairs that I have made a pot of oatmeal." He raised a hand. "Spare me your thoughts on oatmeal."

Sam rubbed her eyes. "Have you heard from Mother?"

"She called about two this morning. She arrived safely and will call back this evening. Feet on the floor, please."

Sam sat up and swung her legs to the side of the bed. "I'm up. See you at the old Treadmill." She waited until he was at the door. "Have a nice daaaay."

He lurched as if shot, then limped into the hall.

Sam giggled. Her father had a thing about "have a nice day." People said it wherever he went, like cuckoos coming out of clocks. Even her mother. "Have a nice daaaay," she would call in a high-pitched voice as he left for school, and he would go into his shot-in-the-back routine.

Have a nice day.

Sam sat immobile, all laughter gone. It was very well to pretend that today was like every other day, and last night only a dream, but real was real. Real was her grandmother having a heart attack and her mother going to Santa Barbara. Real was Bogie Benson. A real parrot was sitting this very minute in the garage studio under one of her mother's discarded tablecloths. A stolen parrot. A parrot important enough to have warranted a special assembly.

Sam showered and dressed with a speed that would have astonished her mother. Tearing downstairs, she grabbed a sweater and sprinted across the driveway and up the studio stairs. Hesitating with one hand on the doorknob, Sam braced herself for a torrent of abuse. When the door swung open to total silence, she approached the cage with growing apprehension. Supposing El Loro had collapsed from all the excitement? Supposing he was dead? Gingerly lifting the cover, she jumped as if someone had lifted her by the hair.

"Beer, beer, beer!" screeched the parrot, nipping viciously at the bars. His incessant squawking pierced Sam's eardrums as she filled his seed cup. "Be quiet! I'm trying to help you—you hear?"

"Beer, beer, beer!"

"And you're not going to get any beer. Water, maybe, if you behave yourself." Sam crept closer. The parrot gave her a puzzled frown, head tilted to one side. Securing the seed cup was no problem, but when she reached for the water cup his beak flew down again. Sam slapped the top of the cage. "Stop that!"

Seeds flew. "Beer, beer, beer!"

Sam stood still, a lump lodging itself in her throat. What must it have been like, caged in a locker room, tormented by a bunch of stupid, insensitive boys? How must it feel to have to fight off everyone who came near you? Sam wished she didn't have to give him back to Bogie today. He needed some tender loving care.

She shook herself. El Loro was trouble with a capital T, and the sooner Bogie came and got him the better. Sam closed the door behind her and started down the stairs, pausing on the bottom step to listen. No sound came from the studio. Sighing with relief, she began running towards the house, only to be startled by the sound of Murray's voice.

"My, my, what a busy girl we are this morning. Did you find what you were looking for in the studio?"

Sam put on her plastic smile. "Nobody ever finds anything up there. Even Mother has given up."

"Ahh—an exercise in futility." He seemed in no hurry. "I am gratified to see that Lucy delivered you to and fro last night without breaking any bones."

Sam squirmed. Ever since last night it was necessary to think twice before answering people. First her father and now Murray. Did it take a special talent to be evasive, like playing the clarinet without squeaking? She spread her arms wide. "I am all in one piece. See?"

"It must have been an interesting ride."

"Not half as interesting as standing out here in the cold talking to you, Murray. Or being late for school. Being late for school is terribly interesting. Or don't you think so, Murray?"

He waggled a crutch at her. "Not quite your style, Samantha, but a creditable performance all the same. Any news?"

"Mother arrived all right. She'll call tonight." Sam ran to the back door and deliberately let it slam. The kitchen seemed out of focus. How long had Murray been standing in the driveway before she had come down those stairs? Had he heard all the squawking and screeching? Even if he hadn't, he must have thought things were pretty odd.

Oh, why did she always have to rise to Murray's bait? Why couldn't she be cool and calm under pressure? Thank heaven she wouldn't have to worry much longer. Bogie would pick up El Loro this afternoon and it would be over. He had promised.

When Sam got off the bus, she saw Bogie leaning against a tree, waiting. He couldn't get near her, though, because Murray was sticking like a burr. Sam stumbled from class to class until, miraculously, Bogie appeared at her elbow at lunchtime.

"Walk out to the Rock with me?"

Sam's heart boomed all the way. She didn't know if it was because Bogie was going to tell her he was taking El Loro off her hands, or because he was going to tell her he wasn't. Sam didn't look at him until they were standing by the rock, and then wished she hadn't.

"Here's the thing," he began. "I'm being *watched.* And what with Seth being so nervous and all, he's likely to start leaking at the mouth."

"But, Bogie—I—you—"

"I need you, Sammie Lou. If they catch me with that paranoid parrot, they'll expel me."

And there would go the big game.

"He's safe with you for a few more days. No one in their right mind would suspect *you* of hiding El Loro."

No one in her right mind would hide El Loro.

Bogie took her hand. "You'll be doing it for the good of old Treadwill. They can't win that game without me. Honest."

37

"I can't— My—my father's been appointed faculty adviser." Sam faltered, the pleading look in his eyes turning her legs to wet macaroni. "But, well—maybe. For—for the good of old Treadwill. But you've got to—"

"Don't worry. I'll come around to check on him every day." He squeezed her hand. "I knew you wouldn't let me down, Sammie Lou."

Sam could have stood basking in his smile forever, except it was only an afterglow. One minute he was there and the next he was hoofing across the lawn with Seth Harper, who had appeared out of nowhere. Sam blinked. The quad was empty. Where had everyone gone? Then she remembered that it was lunchtime.

The thought of eating caused her stomach to roll. She would sit on the Rock and think. Turning to hoist herself up, she bumped smack into someone.

"Hi," Lucy Adams said with a careless shrug. "Nice work Tuesday night—hitching a ride with our hero, I mean."

Sam couldn't let Lucy know how scared she was. "How could you forget to pick me up, Lucy?"

"I didn't forget. I was just busy." She smiled her cherub's smile. "What was in the box?"

"What box?"

"The one between you and Bogie Benson. I saw you as I was cruising away from the Crumbler."

Sam groped for words. It was hard, lying without actually telling a lie. "Oh, that! Just some stuff Bogie was hauling from the locker room."

Lucy blinked her violet eyes. "Well, if you want him back, luv, put yourself between him and the box next time."

Sam made her eyes go slitty. "You should talk to Murray about an Advice for the Lovelorn column, Lucy."

38

"It's biological. You know." Lucy yawned. "Or do you?"

This time it was Sam who left someone standing. She spent the rest of the day trying to avoid everyone, but Murray the Meddler cornered her during the last period and said, "Bill Everett will give us a ride at four thirty."

Sam wanted to tell him she didn't care if Bill Everett would give them a ride to the moon in a silver spaceship. But she *did* have Pep Band. And a ride was a ride. "It sounds enthralling."

It wasn't. It was almost as scary as Lucy. Murray was no more than settled in the car when he said, "I've been thinking about that studio at your place, Samantha."

Sam's heart plummeted like an elevator with a broken cable. "Whatever for?"

"It would make a really good darkroom."

"You're the one who's interested in photography, not me."

"I know. I may ask your folks if they'll rent it to me for a small stipend."

"You can't do that," Sam blurted. "I mean— I'm going to fix it up myself— A place of my own."

"But that won't be until you're grown up, Samantha."

Sam seethed the rest of the way home. The phone was ringing as she unlocked the door.

"What did he say?" Heather asked.

Sam feigned ignorance. "Who?"

"I saw Bogie corner you at the Rock. Did Bogie the Villain outdo Samantha the Guileless? What dastardly scheme has he perpetrated now?"

"For heaven's sake stop being dramatic, Heather!"

"What did he say?"

Sam hated to tell her. She wouldn't tell her. Nothing could make her tell her. She told her.

"They're watching him! They should have been watching him down at the Passion Pit with Phyll Morton last night."

Sam swallowed. "Oh. Did you go to the movies last night?"

"With my mother. She had the hoo-hahs. I think she got the gin and the Valium mixed up again, if you know what I mean."

Sam did and didn't. Everyone knew that Heather's mother had problems; they weren't anything new. "Was she all right?"

"After I walked her around for a while and got a thermos of coffee down her. She giggled a lot." Heather hiccoughed. "It was a very sad movie."

"I'm sorry." Sam was, but what could she do? Heather's mother was Heather's mother. "Listen, wait until I tell you about Murray. And Lucy. I'm getting so jumpy I vault into the ceiling if someone so much as looks at me."

Heather listened, chewing her nails into the mouthpiece. "Tell the truth. You have a guilty conscience."

"I have to go." Sam hung up and sat in a chair. It was depressing, because she had no more than sat down when she realized that she had to feed El Loro before her father came home. The parrot was strangely quiet, almost morose. "Welcome to my world," Sam murmured.

As she filled the cups, he responded by pecking softly at the bars. Sam leaned down and whispered through them. "I know how you feel." A cage was a cage, whether it had real bars or invisible ones. "Listen, I'll teach you a new word. *Honey. Honey. Honey.* Come on. Say hunnn-eeee."

He stared with bleak eyes, then began to eat. Not with his usual speed, but as if waiting for something to happen.

That's what I'm doing, Sam thought as she prepared supper. *Waiting for something to happen, yet hoping noth-*

40

ing does, because whatever it is, it's bound to be trouble.
She was glad when her father came home.

Sam had only eaten a bite or two when she realized her stomach felt funny. Her stomach had been feeling funny all day. Maybe it was the beef Stroganoff in-a-box she'd fixed the night before. Her father seemed to be feeling touches of it, too.

"What is this thing I am eating?" A limp string dangled from his fork.

"Romanoff noodles with parmesan cheese in-a-box."

"Maybe it would be better from now on if you left out the box."

They ate some ice cream.

Sam was helping her father with the dishes when Bogie called. He was sorry, but he couldn't pick up El Loro the next day. He was in a real hassle. "The coach has put everyone on curfew until that lousy parrot shows up."

"But—"

"Take my word for it, Sammie. This is no time to show up with that bird. Just hang on and I'll see what I can do."

Sam couldn't very well argue, with her father standing right by the kitchen phone. "See you tomorrow."

"Sure thing. And don't worry. No one is going to suspect *you*." His voice dropped. "Not my Sammie Lou."

Sam was undecided whether her heart would melt or break. She went back and picked up the dish towel.

Her father said, "I'll stop on my way home tomorrow and buy some more ice cream."

10

"Why the face of gloom?" Sam's father asked across the Mexican casserole a week later. "Dinner's fine. You're getting better with the boxes all the time."

"It was learning to parboil them a few minutes before adding the ingredients that did it."

"I like the macaroni and cheese box best of all. It has a superior brand of cardboard."

Sam managed a feeble smile. "Maybe I should try gourmet dinners. I must have counted a dozen different kinds in the frozen food section today."

"What kind of boxes do *they* come in?"

"They're in plastic bags that you drop right into a pan of boiling water."

"Is the plastic flavored or plain?"

When Sam didn't answer, he plodded cheerfully on. "The news tonight from your mother was great, wasn't it? At least your grandmother is out of the cardiac unit and into a room of her own."

Sam nodded. Her mother had sounded hopeful, almost herself again. And Sam truly was happy that Grandmother Harrington had improved so much.

"The phone again— I'll get it." Sam dragged her feet. It was probably Murray calling to ask how her grandmother was doing. "Hello."

"Is it a private funeral or shall I dress in black?"

"Sorry, Heather." Sam was glad she was in the study where her father couldn't hear her. "I'm in the pits."

"Is your grandmother worse?"

"Actually, she's much better. It's just—oh—I don't know."

"It's been raining for two days and nights and your mother is gone. You are a lousy parboiler of boxes. Bogie still has bandages over his eyes where you are concerned. And then there's the Unwanted Boarder, the Horror, El Loro."

"He almost bit me on the lip this morning."

"What were you doing with your lip that close?"

"Teaching him to kiss me." Sam waited for Heather's horse laugh, but it didn't come.

"You like him!"

"Okay, I like him. If people had treated him right, he wouldn't be such a miserable creature."

"That shows real class, Sam." Heather paused. "For what it's worth on the brighter side, Bogie and Phyll had a fight last night. Rumor has it she walked out on him at the Crumbler."

"Are you sure it wasn't the other way around?"

"It came straight from Lucy Adams."

"Lucy Adams lies a lot."

"Not this time. Bogie and Phyll are busted apart. Doesn't that cheer you?"

There weren't too many people trying to cheer Sam these days. "Is that why you called?"

"No. I wanted to ask you if you could come over and study with me." Heather's usually flat voice went high and catchy. "My mother's gone to a—a meeting."

Was it Sam's imagination Heather sounded lonely? But Heather was used to staying alone. Still, it was better than

43

staying home and worrying about El Loro. "Be there in a few minutes."

"Where?" her father asked.

"I'm going over to study with Heather."

He grinned. "Have a nice eeeevening."

"Ouch." Starting for the stairs, Sam heard the phone ring again. "Get it, will you Daddy?"

Sam was on the third step from the bottom when she heard the magic words, "It's for you, Sam. Bogie Benson."

It was unreal. Walking downstairs when her heart had stopped beating. Talking in a normal voice when a giant valve had closed in her throat. "Bogie?"

"Listen, Sammie," he said without preamble, "Phyll and I have split."

Sam said, "I'm sorry," which she didn't mean.

"Don't be. She was getting to be a drag."

"Oh."

"I've been thinking about you a lot lately, Sammie. All the neat times we used to have. You being such a good egg about El Loro and all. Would you maybe like to go to a movie? I could be over there in eight minutes flat."

Sam could kill herself. Why had she told Heather she would come over? It would be easy to call and cancel. Still, she had said she would go. And a girl shouldn't be too eager when a boy as popular as Bogie asked for a last-minute date. "I'm sorry, I already have plans."

"Oh." He sounded deflated. "How about tomorrow night?"

"I—I thought you were on curfew?"

"Not since we clobbered Jefferson Friday night."

"Well—I guess tomorrow night will be okay."

"The usual time?"

"Sure." Sam hung up. It took considerable concentration to keep from floating upstairs.

44

Her father met her going down. "Sure, what?"

"Bogie Benson asked me to go to a movie tomorrow night."

"Tomorrow's a school night."

"Tonight's a school night, too, but you don't mind my going over to Heather's." Sam picked up her books but something in her father's face stopped her. "Please, Daddy."

"I'll make an exception this time. But no more, agreed?"

"Lots of girls date on school nights."

"You are not lots of girls." He hesitated for only a second. "And Bogie Benson is not lots of boys."

"No! He's just about the greatest, most popular guy on campus, that's all!"

"So I have heard."

Sam walked the block in a swivet. If Bogie should start dating her again, after all of those torturous weeks, was her father going to ruin everything? She was fifteen, almost fifteen and a half. She would be getting her driver's license in another few months. If a girl was old enough to drive a car, why wasn't she old enough to date on school nights?

Heather opened the door before Sam knocked. "I've made some tea."

"What happened to the hot chocolate?"

"I'm giving it up. The old you-can-do-anything-if-only-you-think-you-can."

"You are funny, Heather."

"*You* are glowing, Sam. Did El Loro finally kiss you?"

"Bogie Benson asked me to go to a movie."

"Holy Toledo. I'm glad, Sam."

"Cut it out. You don't like him and you know it."

"Okay. But I'm still glad for *you.*"

Sam wished for the old Heather back. "Aren't you making any dire predictions? Like he broke off with me once, so he could do it again?" Sam stirred her tea slowly. "I've given that some thought. And he *could*. And he could just be trying to be nice to me because I've been keeping El Loro—"

"Or he really could want to take you to a movie." Heather smiled. "What does it matter? You've got a date with him. Don't ask yourself why or worry if there'll be a next. Take it a day at a time."

"You sound like the chaplain in an old war movie."

"Let's study."

An hour and a half passed. Heather's head was buried in her history book, although she hadn't turned a page. As for herself, Sam couldn't think about anything but going out with Bogie again. What should she wear? Thank heaven she didn't have anything extracurricular after school tomorrow. She could wash her hair. She could wear the pearl ring her parents had given her for her last birthday.

Hearing a car in the driveway, Sam glanced at her watch. "Nine thirty. I'd better scoot."

"No!" Heather got up so fast she upset her stool. "It's my mother."

They went into the hall together.

Mrs. Grayson—she always came back to Mrs. Grayson no matter how many men she married—was standing uncertainly in the light from the front porch. She stepped inside, waving gaily. "Hi, angels. What have you been up to?"

Sam smelled the perfumey blast of gin. "I was just leaving."

Heather reached a hand to her teetering mother. "Come out to the kitchen, Mother. I'll make some coffee."

"I don't want any coffee," her mother pouted, pulling away. "I want a little—"

46

Heather's face was a sickly pink, yet she spoke in her best dancing-school voice. "Thanks for coming, Sam. See you tomorrow."

"Sure." Sam made an attempt to pass Mrs. Grayson. "Excuse me—"

Mrs. Grayson's face wore a Silly Putty smile as she clutched Sam's arm. "I declare, Sam, you get prettier every day." She fixed her bleary eyes on Heather. "Isn't Sam just about the most beautiful girl you ever saw, luv?"

Heather laughed her horse laugh. "Some things never change, Mother."

Sam managed to free herself. Walking home in the cool darkness, the air still wet from the rain, she was filled with mixed emotions. Embarrassed for Heather, and ashamed of Mrs. Grayson. How did Heather stand it? She never complained or told other people her troubles. She didn't get all bent out of shape like some girls would. But then, Sam told herself, Heather was *used* to it. That was bound to make it easier.

"I'll put it out of my mind," Sam said aloud. "It's too depressing."

Besides, she had troubles of her own. Not only El Loro, but Bogie Benson. Having him ask her for a date wasn't enough. This time she had to find a way to keep him. No matter what.

If only someone would tell her how!

11

Sam sat in Bogie's Ford in front of her house the next afternoon, wondering if maybe she were dreaming. It was Indian summer, with just a hint of smoke in the air—a slaphappy, pluperfect day for a girl who had never felt slaphappier. Bogie Benson was sitting beside her looking as if he never wanted to leave. In fact, he was counting the beads in her bracelet as if they were gold coins, his finger lingering over each one with a touch that made Sam's head reel.

Did she dare? The question had come to her lips several times during the day, but somehow none of them seemed the right time. But now Bogie had stopped counting and encircled her wrist with his hand, looking at her with those eyes that were exactly the color of iced tea. "A penny," he said.

"I was just thinking—would you like to go to the Backwards Dance with me?"

"I thought you'd never ask," he answered, without letting go of her wrist.

"I—I thought someone else would have asked you by now."

"Phyll? I told you, that's cooled. It'll be like old times, Sammie Lou, going to a dance together." He lowered his voice. "And don't forget we're going to a movie tonight."

How could she forget? "I won't. I—I guess I'd better go in."

He reached across to open the door, gave a short wave, and took the Ford thundering down the street. Sam stood, breathless as always with the sheer unpredictability of Bogie Benson.

Sam went straight through the house and settled herself in a lawn chair in the backyard, stretching her arms to the sky. Nothing seemed real. It was all happening too fast. Was she really Bogie Benson's girl again? "Oh, what a beautiful day," she murmured.

"To what may I attribute this dazzling display of happiness?" Murray asked, coming through the gate. "Never mind. Just let me say it is a welcome change from the blanket of gloom you have been spreading around lately."

Sam knew the day was foolproof when she was glad to see Murray. "Oh—I don't know— Everything seems so special."

"Meaning Bogie Benson, of course."

"Who said anything about Bogie Benson?"

"There is a glaze of idiocy in your eyes that has been noticeably absent of late."

"You can't put me down today, Murray, so don't try."

"What happened to the fair Phyllis? Did someone put poison in her Pepsi bottle? Just who tossed whom aside like an empty Colonel Sanders bucket?"

"You're the editor of the scandal sheet. You tell me."

"Come on, Samantha. Your smile is too smug to be convincing."

Sam got up. "As I have said before, Murray, you pay entirely too much attention to the petty details of my life."

He leaned back with a cat grin. "Nice to have the old

Samantha back. I was about to drown in all of the nubile ecstasy."

"Excuse me, please. I have to wash my hair." She held her back stiff as she walked to the back door. Let Murray have his fun. It was the date with Bogie that mattered. Sam was opening the screen when she heard him call, "How's Heather?"

"What do you mean, how's Heather?"

"She wasn't at school today. Or hadn't you noticed?"

Sam had and she hadn't. She had ridden to school with her father because of an appointment with her guidance counselor, and after that, Bogie had occupied most of her time and thoughts. "She was all right when we studied together last night. I'll give her a call."

Her father was in the kitchen, glasses perched precariously on his nose. "When pork is done," he read from the label on a Chinese dinner box, "add these precious vegetables."

"You're making that up."

"Go away, little girl." He flourished a bottle of soy sauce. "Can't stand little girls in the kitchen when I am trying my hand at the culinary arts. There's a good little girl."

Relieved, Sam went to call Heather. Waiting through several rings, she tried to remember when Heather had last missed a day of school. It was in third grade, the time her mother had accidentally spilled a pot of hot coffee on her shoulder. When Heather finally answered, her voice was far away and listless. "Where were you today?" Sam asked.

"I didn't feel well. Probably withdrawal symptoms from kicking the hot chocolate habit." She laughed a gleeless laugh. "Or maybe I'm allergic to tea."

"You sound peculiar."

50

"Everyone sounds peculiar when they're trying to kick the habit."

"Cut it out. I want to know what's the matter."

"I'll tell you if you don't interrupt." There was a long pause. "I drank a lot of gin last night. It tasted like Chanel Number 5. I couldn't stand up, but when I lay down the bed wouldn't lay down with me. I hung onto the springs and shut my eyes. Oh, and I threw up. But that was later."

Sam was in shock. "Did your mother wake up?"

"No way." And suddenly it was the old Heather, presto digitalis, as Sam's father would say. The flat voice, the familiar horse laugh. "Stop worrying. I feel hunky-dory. Tell me, how's the Horror, El Loro?"

"El Loro's getting tamer every day. All he needed was a little TLC."

"Someone should bottle Tender Loving Care and give out free samples to the whole world." Heather sighed, then said softly, "Have a good time with Bogie tonight, Sam."

"What are you going to do?"

"Go for a bus ride with Murray."

Sam swallowed her surprise. "Where to?"

"A meeting." There was the sound of muted nibbling. "Murray says I need a change of scenery."

Sam didn't know why she was bothered, but she was. After all, *she* was Heather's best friend, wasn't she? Still, Heather and Murray had always had this thing going. The old buddy system, without violins. "Will you tell me about it tomorrow?"

"Sure. We'll exchange vows."

Poor, Heather, Sam thought as she hung up. She should be going out with some super boy like Tom Hanson, instead of riding a bus to a meeting with Murray Howell.

It made Sam feel guilty, having a date with the most popular boy in school.

51

12

"But Daddy!" Sam protested. "No one goes to indoor movies."

"Your mother and I attended one just before she left."

"I mean no one *my* age."

"Nonsense. There are Cinema One and Cinema Two and numerous other theaters which cater to the youth of today."

"But I'm a sophomore now. I could understand if I were still a freshman, but—"

"The answer is no."

"Don't you trust me?"

"I trust you."

"But you don't trust Bogie Benson. That's it, isn't it? You'd let me go if it was Pete Jamieson or some other guy."

"Not true. It's just that I have considerable knowledge of what it is to be young, however doubtful that may seem to you at the moment." A note of exasperation crept into his voice. "Take it on faith. I know more than you do, Sam."

"I thought I was supposed to enrich my life with a variety of relationships—"

"Don't throw my own words at me." He rubbed a hand over his eyes. "And don't think you can get around me. I said no and the answer is no."

"Holy Toledo," Sam exploded. "You'd think we were going to have an orgy or something."

"The subject is closed."

"I'll die!" she wailed. "How can I tell a Big Man on Campus like Bogie Benson my father won't let me go to a drive-in!"

"You'll think of something."

When it came right down to it, Sam did. "The drive-in is a no no," she told Bogie the minute she was settled into the Ford. "And I have to be in by midnight. I know it's the pits and if you want to back out just say so."

"No problem. It might be fun to go to a regular movie." He pulled away from the curb with a sudden burst of speed. "How about that? Your old man suspecting me of ulterior motives."

Sam wanted to tell him that her father was not her "old man," but she'd given him enough no nos for one evening. She gave an exaggerated roll of her eyes. "You know how impossible grown-ups can be."

"Don't I? If my old man isn't breathing down my neck, Coach Gilmore is." He waved at some boys lounging on a corner. "You still like westerns?"

Sam had never liked westerns. "Anything you want is all right with me."

"There's a John Wayne double feature at the Mausoleum."

The Mausoleum, as kids called it, was an ornate old Fox theater that had recently been restored and reopened. "That sounds like fun."

Once inside the theater, Sam clung to Bogie's hand until they had climbed to the last row of seats in the empty balcony. She supposed there were people downstairs, yet it seemed she was alone with Bogie in the false darkness. The whirring film followed a yellow shaft over their heads and onto the screen below. Sam thought of her father and his worry about drive-ins, and giggled. "I've never sat up so high before."

"I don't like people breathing down my neck." Bogie propped his feet on the seat in front of him and folded his arms across his chest. "Okay, Duke. Up and at 'em."

Sam nibbled popcorn one kernel at a time, stealing glances at Bogie's profile to make sure it wasn't all a dream. Oh, the sheer bliss of sitting beside him, of getting a second chance! Shutting the movie out of her mind, Sam vowed never to take anyone for granted again.

Bogie sat up, squirmed, and stretched his arm around her. Just as Sam was wondering if she should move closer, he solved the dilemma by giving her a decisive pull. Her head landed snugly onto his shoulder. It was as firm and strong as she remembered.

In the next hour, between bites of popcorn they fed to each other, Sam was kissed three times on the mouth. During the intermission, Bogie took her down to the lobby and bought peanuts and two paper cups of cola. It was tricky not spilling her drink as they made the long climb back to the balcony. Not that Sam cared. It was being with Bogie that mattered. Being close to him, kissed up there, high in the darkness.

Walking to the car after the movie, everything seemed larger than life, brighter and more garish than Sam remembered. She spent some delicious moments wondering if Bogie was going to take her up to the Point, where all the kids went to make out. She spent some scary moments wondering what she would do if he did.

He pulled in at McDonald's. "You want a Big Mac?"

"No, thanks." Sam was full of popcorn, peanuts, and cola. And something else. Something that filled her chest like a balloon that someone was blowing up ever so slowly.

"Just a root beer, please."

"What kind of socks are those?"

"Crazy."

"Wow."

Sam was glad she had worn the zigzag crazies. Phyllis Morton might have blonde hair and a truly spectacular bosom, but her legs weren't as good as Sam's. And she didn't have Bogie Benson anymore. At least not for tonight. Sam shivered.

"You want to go for a ride?" Bogie kissed her. "Relax. I'll get you home before your old man sends out the marines."

Over his shoulder, Sam saw Lucy Adams' Trans Am whizz past and grind to a stop beside them. She didn't know the boy in front with Lucy, but the one in back with Phyll Morton was definitely Fairview's first-string quarterback.

Lucy waved an erratic hand, her voice slurring. "Oh, goodie! Sam and Bogie! Where's the box?"

"What box?" Bogie asked.

"The one that stopped the fun and games."

Bogie reached for the ignition. "You sound a bit sauced."

Lucy giggled. "We scrounged a couple of six packs. You want some?"

"I'm in training."

"What for?" Phyll called from the back seat.

Bogie backed out and into the street. He drove without speaking. His face had lost its blackness and in its place was a cool, almost rigid calm. "Don't let them bug you. Phyll thinks she can make me jealous by bumming around with that Fairview jock, and Lucy Adams is a tramp."

55

"They don't bug me," Sam lied.

They were on the outskirts of town when Bogie's foot suddenly jammed to the floor, sending the Ford into a burst of whining speed. Sam clutched the edge of her seat, pushing against the upholstery. As they careened along, headlights cutting the night into jigsaw pieces, Sam stole a glance at the boy beside her. The Bogie she knew was gone. In his place was a stranger who was fighting the world with his Ford. Sam opened her mouth and closed it again.

When in a crisis situation, keep quiet, or so her mother had always told her. Was this a crisis situation? Sam hoped not. Still, the speedometer was jumping around 90. Seeing headlights approach, Sam automatically braced herself. The oncoming car veered sharply, horn blaring.

Bogie swore softly, one eye on the rearview mirror. "Oh-oh."

The car he had crowded off the road had turned around and was speeding after them, horn still blowing. As it gained ground, Bogie yelled, "Hang on!" and swung into a side road. The car rocked wildly in loose dirt, almost over-turning, then sped forward again only to come to a dead end. Bogie screeched to a halt, his shoulders slumping. "Of all the rotten luck! Don't say anything. Leave this to me."

The car pulled to a stop behind them. A man got out and walked to Bogie's window. "Out, mister."

Bogie said, "Hey, look. I'm okay, you're okay. What's the hassle?"

"Out."

Bogie slid from beneath the wheel and stood in the glare of the headlights.

"Just as I thought. A kid." The man pushed a hat to the

56

back of his head, hand shaking. "You realize you could have killed somebody? Speeding— Driving on the wrong side of the road—"

"I'm sorry."

"You're *sorry?*" The man took a pad and pencil and began writing down Bogie's license number. "I've got a wife and baby back there. My wife's in a state of panic. You could have killed us all."

The thought of a baby being injured started a drumming in Sam's ears. She heard the man ask, "You been drinking?"

"No, sir. I just have a heavy foot sometimes." Bogie gave the man a boyish grin. "My pop'll kill me if he hears about this."

"You won't have to wait for your pop if you keep on driving like that. You've got a girl in there! Don't you care if you kill someone's daughter or not?"

A baby's cry shattered the air.

"I wish you wouldn't turn me in." Bogie tugged at his wallet, showing his driver's license. "I'm a careful driver. Look—I don't have any citations."

The man's face was a riddle as he put the pad back into his pocket. "All right. But I'm keeping your number. I'm expecting you to show up at my place next week. You can mow the lawn or anything else as long as it's work."

"It'll have to be a Sunday, sir," Bogie told him. "I play football, and—"

"I don't hold with working on Sundays." The man stared at Bogie. "But you show up in church Sunday morning and I'll tear up your number. That's the Baptist, on South Street."

"Yes, sir. What time, sir?"

"Eleven." He turned to go. "Bring your girl if you like.

57

My wife and I would be glad to have you stay for Sunday dinner."

Sam found her voice. "I—I go to Faith Lutheran."

"That's okay," Bogie said. "I'll be there." Only when the man's taillights had disappeared did he get back into the Ford. "I sure lucked out on that one."

Sam's body felt as if it had turned to Jell-O. "Ooooh—" Bogie began to laugh. "My Pop would die if he knew I was going to church. He says a guy can get bald from sitting in damp churches."

Sam heard a high-pitched giggle and realized it had come from her own throat.

"You are some girl," Bogie marveled.

"You are some idiot."

"I just like to blow out the carbon now and then."

"You nearly blew it, period."

"Come on. You never turned a hair."

Sam was about to tell him she didn't have any hair left to turn when it occurred to her she should play it as it lay. If Bogie thought she was cool, that was what it was all about. Proving to him she was his kind of girl. Ignoring her melting bones, she said, "You sure know how to handle a car."

He reached for her, and they rode into town in silence. Parking in front of her house, Bogie jerked upright as the porch light came on. "Tomorrow night?"

"I'm sorry. I can't date on week nights anymore."

A soft blast escaped his lips. "Friday then? After the game?"

Sam's heart swelled. "All right."

Walking her up the steps, he kissed her, with one eye on the door. "See you."

Sam was afraid to move for fear she would splinter with

58

happiness. Friday night was *game* night. That meant she was Bogie's girl again, for sure. She opened the door in a dreamy motion and saw her father standing in the hall in his robe and pajamas. "You didn't have to wait up for me—"

"You didn't have to come home on time, either." He bent to kiss her, then began climbing the stairs.

It occurred to Sam how tired he must be. If she hadn't stayed out until midnight, he would probably have gone to bed much earlier. If only he had *trusted* her!

She was in her room when it hit her. Her father had reason these days not to trust her, for the first time in his life. Not only was she hiding a stolen parrot, she had been out with a boy who had driven recklessly and nearly gotten into trouble over it. Sam was glad her mother wasn't home. Her mother would have noticed something was wrong.

Later, Sam stopped brushing her teeth and stared into the mirror. She could keep Bogie this time, even if she wasn't as sophisticated as Phyll Morton. Even if her father was living in the Dark Ages where dating was concerned. All she had to do was remember to play it cool. The way she had tonight.

Sam fell asleep thinking about Bogie going to the Baptist church on Sunday. Eating dinner with that man and his wife, maybe even playing with the baby. She couldn't make any of it come into focus. Bogie belonged on the football field. Running. Throwing. Lounging in the halls with the members of the team. Sitting in the back row of the auditorium with the *big* Seniors. Dancing at the Crumbler with his best girl, basking in the smiles, the worshipping glances. Getting his picture in the paper.

So he drove a little fast. He hadn't killed anyone, had

59

he? And he was sorry. Otherwise he would have given that man trouble. He had taken his punishment like a man.

And why not? He was a hero, wasn't he?

13

"How was it?" Heather asked on the bus the next morning. "Going out with Mr. Big again."

"Fantastic." Sam was glad Murray had elected to sit in back and study. "I have a date with him after the game Friday."

Heather whistled. "My stars and garters! Are you keeping score?"

"Trying to." Sam wanted to confide in Heather about the wild ride and the man they'd crowded off the road, but thought better of it. "How was *your* evening?"

"Very enlightening." Heather gave her familiar horse laugh. "Riding a bus with Murray is fine. He reads street signs backwards. Even the driver was—"

"Snore."

"How often have *you* seen a bus driver laughing?" Heather paused. "I mean, evirD dribgnikcoM?"

"What?"

"Mockingbird Drive."

Sam rolled her eyes. "You promised we would exchange

vows. You still haven't told me where you were going on the bus with Murray. Can you come over tonight and talk?"

Heather pretended to be studying a date book. "It just so happens I am free tonight. I am free every night this week except Tuesday and Thursday."

"I envy you. *Your* mother doesn't care if you date on school nights."

"It's not dating. I'll tell you about it tonight."

"Sure." Was Heather going for more bus rides with Murray? But why Tuesdays and Thursdays? "Have you joined a club?"

"Something like that."

"With Murray?"

"He goes along for the ride."

"Reading streets signs backwards?" Sam sighed. "Now you really have me guessing!"

The bus stopped and Sam heard Murray's voice at her elbow.

"Exit time. The world is waiting."

Sam flashed a plastic smile only to find he was looking at Heather.

Heather smiled. "Another day, another twenty-four hours."

Murray gave her a conspiratorial grin and turned to Sam. "You look positively radiant, Samantha. Did you eat Sunshine Snaps for breakfast?"

"With sugar and cream." Sam didn't move. Bogie was waiting by the tree—would she ever get used to it?—And she was blast if she was going to let Murray follow her off the bus with his x-ray eyes. Yet when she finally descended the steps, Murray had cornered Bogie, and all she could do was walk on past.

61

Bogie caught up with her in the quad. "Why didn't you wait for me?"

"You seemed busy."

"Only Old Hobble. He's getting a bunch of football pictures together for the big game issue of the paper and—"

"Hobble?"

"You know."

"His name is Murray."

"Sure." Bogie scowled. "Or maybe you'd rather I called him Mr. Howell?"

Sam felt a kind of panic. Why was she making him mad? With a quick smile, she handed him her books. "That's great. About the pictures for the paper."

Bogie's grin was back. "I'd like to drive you home after school again, or has that been declared out of bounds, too?"

"What about football practice?"

"You have Pep Band." He had memorized her schedule!

"We can give it a trial run."

Bogie rubbed his curly brown hair. "What does your father think could possibly happen to his precious daughter in broad daylight in front of his house?"

"Nothing." Sam's heart skipped a beat.

When she opened her locker, he leaned toward her behind the shelter of the door. "Your eyes turn green when you're mad."

"I wasn't mad."

"Yes you were. Just because I called Murray—"

His face was so close Sam had trouble breathing. "Does—does everyone call him that? I mean, the team and all?"

"Who cares?" He kissed her on the mouth.

"Bogie! *Please!*"

Lucy and Phyll walked past, Lucy staring in open admiration. "If you ever need a stand-in, Sam, I am available, day or night."

Color drained from Bogie's face. "Get lost."

Sam closed the locker. The last thing she heard as she squeezed past Bogie was Phyll muttering, "How tacky can you get?"

Walking down the corridor, Sam held herself erect, hoping no one would notice how flustered she was. Why did Phyll Morton always do that to her? No one cared what Lucy Adams thought. But Phyll— Phyll had been Bogie's big passion—

Rounding the corner, she collided with Pete Jamieson. "Oops, I'm sorry."

He bent to retrieve some papers that had flown from her English binder and when he straightened, his head grazed her chin. His own paper scattered along with his notebook. Sam leaned to help, and their heads bumped. Sam giggled. "I should watch where I'm going."

"My fault!" Pete backed away, only to collide with Miss Eaglethorpe. "I'm sorry." Sam moved to let him pass.

"Good morning, Samantha," Miss Eaglethorpe said with a wry smile.

Sam shuffled the tangle of papers. "What a mess!"

"You'll manage." Miss Eaglethorpe inserted her key into the lock of the English room and busied herself at her desk. "How are you coming with the mystery of the missing parrot?"

It gave Sam a start. "I'm afraid I haven't had much time to work on it."

"What a pity. An interesting approach."

Sam was relieved when Heather plunked herself down in the next seat. "Wow!"

"What's wrong?"

"I don't know. Nothing. Everything." Sam stared hopelessly into Heather's eyes. "I just wish people would stop making innocent remarks that send my blood pressure into the stratosphere."

"Guilt complex. Get rid of you-know-who in your garage and you'll feel better."

"It's not just that. Phyll and Lucy were at me again just now. Bogie was kissing me behind my locker door."

"Grandstander."

"Quiet, please," Miss Eaglethorpe cautioned.

Students straggled to their seats in a kind of collective misery. Heather groaned. "I'd give anything if I didn't have to get that Shakespeare exam back."

Sam had forgotten all about the exam. Miss Eaglethorpe called the class to order and began walking down the aisles passing out corrected sheets. There was a neat A+ in the upper righthand corner of Sam's paper. She looked up in time to see Miss Eaglethorpe drop a sheet onto Heather's desk.

"I see I blew another one," Heather said. "I just can't seem to get the hang of Shakespeare."

"If you'd like to come by after class, I'd be happy to go over your paper with you."

"I have Marching Band."

"Oh. Give me a call at home sometime, then? I'm sure I can help you."

Sam waited until Miss Eaglethorpe had passed into the next aisle. "Ugh—spending an evening with old Eagle Eye."

Heather gave a half smile. "I don't mind her. It's the company she keeps. I'll probably stumble over Julius Caesar's fallen body on her front steps."

64

Sam felt better. "You are funny, Heather."

"I know. I am a very funny girl." She waited until Miss Eaglethorpe was back at her desk, then went up to talk to her. Coming back, she whispered, "She's free tonight. Bet you never thought I'd stand you up for a Roman general and a bunch of assassins."

Miss Eaglethorpe frowned. "Quiet, please."

Poor Heather. Sam would be bored silly if she had to spend an evening talking with Miss Eaglethorpe about *Julius Caesar.* Besides, when was she going to find out what was going on between Heather and Murray? How long would she have to wait before Heather unraveled the mystery of the bus rides, and the meetings on Tuesdays and Thursdays?

At breakfast Sam said, "Bogie's driving me home after school. Is that against the rules?"

Her father stared at her over a plate of watery scrambled eggs. "Not as long as you come straight home."

"Thanks." Sam's happiness was short-lived.

"I understand you are going off campus to eat lunch with Bogie."

"Only down the street to the Pizza Place."

"I know it's a broken record," he sighed, "but there is such a thing as seeing too much of one boy at your age. It limits your horizons, puts you in an isolation booth."

Sam tried to think of something more heavenly than being in an isolation booth with Bogie Benson. "I'm not dating him on week nights. We have to eat somewhere, and no one would be caught dead in—"

"—the cafeteria, where they serve dog food."

"Wherever did you hear a thing like that?"

Her father finished his coffee. "You might give the cafeteria another chance."

"Tell the truth, Daddy. Do you honestly like the food in the cafeteria?"

"I take the Fifth." He threw his hands in the air in a gesture of mock surrender. "And okay. You may eat off campus."

Sam felt an out-of-reason joy. She hastily stuffed dishes in the dishwasher. When her father came downstairs, she kissed him and said, "Your tie is crooked."

"Smart aleck."

The minute his car was out of the driveway, Sam rushed to the studio, where she was greeted with El Loro's newly acquired phrase, "Hello honey—"

Sam leaned down for her morning kiss. "*Who's* your honey?"

"Sam Sam Sam."

As she fed him and filled the water cup she paused for an unexpected thought. How she would miss El Loro when he was gone! Which triggered an increasingly worrisome question. How was she going to manage El Loro's departure when the time came without getting caught? She relied on an increasingly comforting answer. Bogie would take care of everything.

Back inside, Sam called Heather. "Wait for me, will you? Maybe we can talk before the bus comes."

"Okay, but hurry."

Heather met her at the door with an egg in one hand and pepper grinder in the other. "Come out to the kitchen."

Sam perched herself on a bar stool while Heather stirred a concoction in a tall glass. "What's that?"

"Pick-me-up. For my mother when she wakes up. She sometimes forgets to eat."

"It looks gross. What's in it?"

"Raw eggs, tomato juice, Tabasco sauce, ground pepper, and a shot glass of lemon juice." Seeing Sam make a face, she added, "It's not that bad. I put it by her bed every morning before I go to school."

Sam decided to change the subject. "How was it at old Eagle Eye's last night?"

"Great. Miss Eaglethorpe has a lot of class."

"If you like quadruple-lens glasses and dangling participles."

"She's different at home. Did you know her mother lives with her? Don't yawn. She's neat. Seventy-two years old and still plays tennis every day. Swims at the Y. Feeds birds on their windowsill, and has plants and flowers in hangers all over the house. Makes her own macrame. Translates Horace." Heather stopped stirring. "She *adores* Miss Eaglethorpe."

Sam had never thought of Miss Eaglethorpe having a mother. "Why do you suppose she never got married? The kids at school say she had a tragic love affair. Can you imagine Miss Eaglethorpe in *love?*"

"Yes. She's beautiful."

"Miss *Eaglethorpe?*"

Heather gave the pick-me-up one last stir and clamped a plastic lid on the glass. "You don't have to have a pretty face or figure to be beautiful. Miss Eaglethorpe is beautiful inside."

Sam was incredulous. "What did you *talk* about?"

"Macrame. Shakespeare and *Julius Caesar*. Oscar Peterson."

"Who's Oscar Peterson?"

"Miss Eaglethorpe says he's the greatest living jazz pianist."

"Get back to *Julius Caesar*. Did she make it any easier?"

"Yes. She made the characters come alive. I had never thought of them as real people—they were just words on a page. But they had real problems, just as we do today."

Sam yawned. "Listen. You promised to tell me about Murray and the bus rides."

Heather glanced at the clock. "We've run out of time— and there might not be anything to tell."

"If you won't tell me, then I'll have to ask Murray!"

"Go ahead." Heather started up the stairs with the glass. "It's time for the bus."

Sam stalked out only to see Murray standing on the corner. "What are you doing catching the bus at Heather's stop?"

"Why isn't Treadwill's hottest pigskin artist picking you up instead of letting you ride the nasty old bus?"

Sam ignored his cat smile. "I wanted to ride the nasty old bus so you could tell me where you and Heather go on those mysterious bus rides every Tuesday and Thursday night."

"I'd have thought you'd know all about that by now."

"How can I know if nobody tells me?"

"Maybe you haven't been doing your homework." He went to meet Heather, and the three of them stood in silence. When the bus came, Sam walked to a back seat. To her dismay, she saw Heather had chosen a seat up front with Murray.

Sam couldn't take her eyes off them. What on earth did Heather have to talk about that kept her staring morosely at her hands? Why was Murray listening as if Heather were revealing state secrets? Not that Murray didn't always listen to people that way. Sam squirmed. *She* was the only person Murray needled. It was a new thought, and immediately brought Sam rising to her own defense. Was it her fault that Murray liked to pick on her, make those jeering jabs?

Still. Heather was confiding in *him,* instead of her. It made Sam feel odd. Why was Heather shutting her out? Weren't they best friends? What were best friends for?

The bus rounded a curve. As the school came into view, Sam caught her breath. The familiar figure was lounging by the tree again, waiting for her. Not Phyll Morton or any other girl in school. Bogie Benson was waiting for *Sam Grant.*

Treadwill trampled Emerson High the next week with Bogie breaking a last-quarter tie in a spectacular run for a touchdown. He insisted that Sam had brought him luck, lifting her off her feet after the game, smelling of sweat and Gatorade.

"Close your eyes."

Sam felt him put a box in her hand. Opening it, she saw a gold football on a chain. "Oh, Bogie—"

He fastened it around her neck. "A little magic for the big game."

"I'll never take it off." Sam thought of how much she loved the games now that Bogie was her steady guy again. Sitting with the Pep Band, playing rally songs while the cheerleaders jumped and the flag corps waved their flags. She loved the lights that turned the stadium into a kaleidoscope of movement and color, the shrill screams of the crowd, and the Marching Band with its sparkle of uniforms and dancing plumes. Sam hugged Bogie. "I'll even wear it to bed. Thank you so much!"

They went to the Crumbler and danced every dance. Sam's heart took a momentary plunge when she saw Lucy and Phyll come in with the same Fairview jocks they'd been with at McDonald's, but all Bogie said was, "Those guys sure like to be seen in enemy territory."

"I hope they don't cause any trouble." Sam leaned close to his ear. "I mean, about El Loro."

"If they wanted that kind of trouble, they'd have brought reinforcements, not girls." Bogie danced Sam by their booth. "Greetings."

"Oh, lookee," Lucy squealed, "our hero!"

Noting the slurriness of her voice, Sam was sure there was something besides Pepsi in those glasses. Bogie circled in place, holding her close. "Come over to find out how the game's played, fellas?"

A ripple slid down Sam's spine as one of the boys half rose from his seat, but the quarterback waved him back.

"You'll find out how the game's played when it's time for the big one—"

Bogie grinned. "Stop scaring me. I'll fold for sure."

"I'd rather you laid a bet. Ten bucks for every point you lose."

Phyll had been sitting with downcast eyes, but now she looked at Bogie with an unreadable smile. "You can't afford to lay bets on anything these days, can you Bogie?"

"I'll lay you a hundred to one the air's polluted in here."

Bogie spun Sam swiftly towards the door, only to meet Murray and Heather coming in. "Hi—"

"Great game," Murray said. "I just told Heather I'm beginning to run out of headlines and she suggested, BATTLING BOGIE DOES IT AGAIN."

"—but Murray topped it with BENSON WINS ANOTHER ONE FOR THE GOAT."

"Thank you, thank you, thank you," Bogie chanted, waving his hand to the floor. "Praise from the peasants is always welcome."

Sam was uneasy. Why was it that Heather never missed an opportunity to needle Bogie? And what was she doing at the Crumbler with Murray Howell, of all people? And Murray, standing there wreathed in smiles as if running into Bogie was the best thing that could have happened to an adoring peasant!

"Has any of the scuttlebutt about the missing parrot been filtering down to the locker rooms, Bogie?" he asked.

"If there was anything new on that crummy bird, I would be the first to know." Bogie groaned. "Yammer, yammer, yammer."

"Then you've heard about the select Committee of Fairview students who have been appointed to snoop around—venerable athletes, all."

71

Bogie gave Sam a broad wink. "Sherlock Holmes' Regulars?"

Murray pressed on. "If my sources are correct, they've found some clues."

"Those snoops of yours couldn't find the School Rock."

"What kind of clues?" Sam asked.

"The kind one gets from traitors."

"You mean—someone from *Treadwill?*"

"Right." Murray moved an elbow to steer Heather aside. "Of course, such people are seldom trustworthy."

"Sounds like more yammer to me," Bogie said, holding the door.

Sam waited until they were safely inside the Ford before she dared speak. "Do you think they know where El Loro is?"

"They don't know anything. Old Hobble is just showing off."

"But what if—?" The possibilities were overwhelming. Sam would be disgraced, maybe expelled. And her father— He would not only be disappointed in her, but furious to boot. "I think I want to go home."

"Don't let those jerks get to you."

"Heather and Murray are not jerks," Sam flared.

"Okay, okay!"

Riding beside him, Sam's tension gradually subsided. How could a boy like Bogie Benson understand a girl like Heather or a boy like Murray? Was it Bogie's fault he had been born with a magic circle around him? And why had she let Murray upset her? If Fairview actually had any clues, wouldn't they have acted on them by now?

Sam snuggled close to Bogie and suddenly they were at the Point, and he was parking on the furthest bluff even though there were no other cars in sight. She tried to concentrate on the town below them, spread out like a carpet of diamonds, while Bogie reached into the glove compartment and pulled out a pack of cigarettes.

"I didn't know you smoked."

"It's a well-kept secret." The lighter flared briefly, outlining his face.

"But—the team—training—"

He gave a hungry pull on the cigarette. "Look. I run faster and throw for more touchdowns than anyone in the crummy Conference League. Where does that put all of their no-smoking, no-drinking, early to bed yammer?"

Sam winced. "Do—do the rest of the team smoke?"

"We win. That's what counts." He gave a short laugh. "Stop worrying, Sammie. No one plays by the rules anymore."

Sam opened her mouth to protest and shut it again. She was a rule breaker, too, wasn't she? Hiding El Loro? Oh, why couldn't things be the way they used to be? No El Loro to worry about, or sneaky scouts from Fairview with their scary clues. Just her and Bogie, without a care in the world?

As if on cue, his arm went around her. "Sammie Lou—"

Along with a sudden leap of Sam's heart came a kind of uneasiness. The closeness of Bogie's face made everything a blur, worsened by the smouldering cigarette in the ashtray. She struggled to reach the window handle. "That smoke—"

His arms tightened. "Relax. It's go-to-hell night."

Sam didn't want to go to hell. She didn't even know how. For all her dreaming of what she would do if she ever had a chance with Bogie again, now that it was here she found herself as painfully unprepared as ever. His cigarette was choking her, so she stubbed it out. "If you want to break the rules, okay. I don't."

Bogie picked up her arms and draped them around his neck. "Where's the fun if you don't break a few rules?"

Cars were now parked all around. Inside them, Sam knew, couples were making out. Why couldn't she? Especially when she had sworn she would do *anything* if she could get Bogie Benson away from Phyll Morton. Did Phyll make out? Sam thought she knew the answer. And if she wanted to keep him, she would have to, too. She decided to try.

It was exciting. Sam had never been kissed in such a way, or held so intimately. She was torn between sensations she had never felt before and her own inbred sense of right and wrong. Everything was happening too fast.

"Shall we get in the back seat? Come on, Sammie—you know I'm crazy about you—"

Sam longed to tell him she was crazy about him, too, but all she could do was stutter, "I think you'd better take me home."

His arms slackened, then let go. With a flick of his wrist, the engine sprang to life and headlights gleamed. Backing out with spinning wheels, Bogie circled the Point at high speed, one hand on the wheel, the other on the horn. Disgruntled yells came from the cars, and horns blew in protest. Bogie responded by flipping the radio to infinity, sending music blaring across the secluded rendezvous.

A boy jumped from a car, arms flailing. "Hey, Benson! Have a heart!"

Bogie slowed to a crawl. "Sorry, friend. Go back to your playpen."

To Sam's relief, he drove towards the lane leading to the highway, but instead of turning, continued in a circle

74

again, still at a snail's pace. A low whistle escaped his teeth. He fumbled for another cigarette, lit it, and inhaled deeply. Around and around they went, slower and slower.

Sam sat numbly, caught in a wordless vacuum. How long would Bogie continue this mindless merry-go-round? She searched his face for a glimmer of glee, a spark of mischief, and saw nothing but blankness, heard nothing but that dreadful whistle. She had blown it. This was her last date with Bogie Benson.

Sam gradually became aware of people in the parked cars. A black Trans Am was all but hidden in a clump of trees, and Sam saw Lucy Adams untangling herself to peer out a window. Phyll Morton's laugh floated through the air. Bogie's foot jammed to the floorboard, the sudden speed hurtling Sam against the seat. The car gained speed as it reached the main highway.

Watching curves appear and disappear, Sam gasped. "Don't go so fast! You're scaring me. Please."

Bogie resumed the maddening crawl. "Better?"

"You don't have to overdo it."

His hands hung over the steering wheel as though broken at the wrists. "First you're with me, then I'm poison. First you want me to slow down, then you say I'm overdoing it. Can't you make up your mind?"

Only a few short minutes ago, Sam had been certain that all she wanted was Bogie Benson. Yet when the chance had come, she'd lost it. "I just want you to drive in the middle. You know. Not too fast. Not too slow."

To her astonishment, he reached for her hand. "You're not just talking about driving, are you?"

"I—I guess not."

"I did come on kind of strong." He smiled ruefully. "I forgot what a nice girl you are, Sammie."

Sam wished she could understand him. The scowling, unpredictable show-off at the Point was gone. In his place was this repentant Bogie who was now saying he was afraid she wouldn't want to go out with him again. Sam gave his hand a small squeeze. "Yes, I will."

"Tomorrow night?"

"All right."

"How about Sunday? Maybe we could have a picnic at Everett's Pond."

Sam hesitated. Everett's Pond was taboo. It was like the Point, only worse. There was an old rowboat there that didn't seem to belong to anyone, and there were plenty of rumors about girls who would get into it and let themselves be rowed over to the tiny island in the middle of the Pond. "I can't, Bogie. I'm going to church with my father, and then over to an aunt's for dinner." Sam felt as glamorous as a plucked chicken. "But maybe you'd like—I mean—would you come to Sunday supper?"

"Sounds like a deal."

"Six o'clock." Sam was unable to believe that everything was all right again. "Is that okay?"

He pulled up in front of her house and cut the motor. "Hey. Your old man hasn't turned on the porch light."

"The Howells invited him over for sandwiches after the game."

Bogie got out without letting go of her hand. Sam slid under the wheel and into his arms. He kissed her, lightly, but not lightly. Sam wished she knew how he did that. However he did it, it was very disturbing, even more so than those feverish kisses up at the Point. Sam's bones seemed to melt into jellied marrow as she walked up the steps.

"Good night, Sammie Lou," Bogie whispered, and was gone.

Sam closed the door and leaned against it. Something nagged at her, jolting her from her state of bliss. She had invited Treadwill's most popular boy to Sunday supper! It must have been temporary insanity. What would a boy like Bogie have to say to her father? And her father! Supposing he already had plans for Sunday night?

The door was pushed open, throwing Sam off balance. "Oh, hi, Daddy."

"Glad I caught you. I talked to your mother after the game tonight, and she had a great idea. When I told her what marvelous weather we're having, she said we should have a cookout. Invite some young people in. What do you say to Sunday evening?" Without waiting for an answer, he went on, "I thought of Heather and Murray, and you'll no doubt want to invite Bogie Benson. Anyone else?"

Who? Things were bad enough before he'd dragged Heather and Murray in. Bogie was sure to drop dead of the yawns. "That—that should be just right."

"Good. I'll pick up some steaks on my way home from golfing tomorrow."

"But, Daddy—kids would lots rather have hamburgers—or even hot dogs."

"It's time we splurged. We haven't eaten anything but junk food since your mother left. And steak is just what the doctor ordered for young football players. Got that straight from Coach Gilmore's mouth."

Sam wanted to run away. Hide. Die. Anything.

"Great having some young people around the house for a change." Her father beamed. "You want some hot chocolate?"

"No, thanks. I think I'll go on up to bed."

Sam felt clammy. She wished her mother were here instead of in Santa Barbara. Her mother knew how to make people feel at ease. Even an odd threesome like Heather, Murray, and Bogie Benson. Sam brushed her teeth and crawled into bed. Oh, why did grown-ups always seem to think that steak solved everything? The jar of the telephone brought her upright and she leaped from bed.

"H-hello—"

"Bogie. How are you?"

"I'm just fine." Sam giggled. "Where are you?"

"In the top bunk of the so-called bedroom."

"Who's in the bottom bunk?"

"My two little brothers."

"I didn't know you had any little brothers!"

"It's not my favorite subject. They're only in kindergarten. My old man didn't know whether to shoot himself or my mother. Eleven years after they had me, and whammo—twins!" Bogie paused with a note of bitterness. "The way they take on now you'd think the double-troubles are going to grow up to be the first twin presidents of the United States."

There was a silence, as if both of them were waiting. Sam decided she would never have a better chance. "There've been some changes made," she said with more than a hint of martyrdom. "Sunday supper has turned into a party. My father thinks it is time the house rang with the joyous cries of youth."

"You sound like Old Hobble," he said, and quickly added, "who's coming?"

"Heather and Murray."

"You call that a party?" But he sounded relieved. "As a

78

matter of fact, my plans have changed, too. There was a note pinned to the old icebox door. I can't keep our date for tomorrow night. I have to twin-sit." He plowed on as though he wanted to get it over with. "It seems Saturday is my folks' eighteenth wedding anniversary."

"You mean you didn't *know*?"

"I don't pay much attention to the yammer going on around here."

"Oh. Well, then, I'll see you Sunday evening."

"I'd ask you to come over and help hold the defensive but my folks think I'm not old enough to be alone with a girl in the house and only a couple of five-year-olds for chaperones."

A crimson tide washed Sam's face. "My father wouldn't let me come anyway."

There was a soft blowing in the receiver. "I just blew you a kiss."

"Thank you."

Sam hung up, touching her lips as if the kiss had actually landed on them. There was a tap on the door. "Yes?"

Her father stuck his head inside. "Who was on the phone?"

"Bogie."

"I thought he just left."

"He did."

"Oh. That explains everything."

Sam tried to hide her annoyance. "He can't take me to the movies tomorrow night. It's his folk's anniversary."

Her father started down the hall. "Nice for families to be together on occasions like that."

Sam heard his door close. Snuggling down in bed, she tried to concentrate on how disappointed she was about the date tomorrow night. Or on how she could possibly

79

manage to have Sunday supper for three of the most unlikely guests a girl would ever have. It wasn't any use. One startling thought kept crowding everything else out of her head.

Bogie Benson. *Baby-sitting!*

16

By Sunday evening, Sam's stomach was alive with fluttering moths. The steaks lay on the countertop in the kitchen, lavishly seasoned with soy sauce and cracked pepper. They looked gruesome. Her father was trying to make a salad dressing, insisting he knew exactly how her mother did it. She stopped to watch, and all at once began to understand.

Her father had said he wanted the joyous cries of youth in the house, but this whole affair was really a mother's day—missing the mother. Sam felt selfish and mean. Her mother had been gone so long, he was bound to miss her. Sam laughed inside, hearing her mother saying, "Your tie is crooked" when her father went to work some mornings.

And that silly joke they had between them when he would call her Charley, and she would say, "My name is not Charley." So cornball—but Sam remembered in her mother's last letter she had written, "No one out here ever calls me Charley." Watching her father go out the back door, Sam decided to make apple crisp, her father's favorite dessert.

A while later, Murray came in the side door. "What's behind the smoke screen out there?"

"My father. He's burning the steaks at the stake."

Murray favored her with a genuine laugh. Heather came up behind him. "Something smells good in here."

"Apple crisp," Sam told her. "I've made it for dessert. It may save the day when my father gets through doing his thing out there." She paused, eyeing Heather. She seemed pale, with a kind of forced gaiety, as if she were wearing a false suit of armor.

Bogie was late. When Sam led him from the side gate into the backyard, he nodded to Heather and Murray, then shook hands with her father in a too hearty fashion. "How are you, sir? Nice to be here."

"Our pleasure," her father responded, turning the steaks.

Heather cleared her throat. "You're in for a treat, Benson. Sam's made apple crisp for dessert."

"—and my father's making steak crisp," Sam quipped.

There was nervous laughter. Sam busied herself at the table, weighting down paper napkins with flatware, laying out an array of relishes and chips. As her father transferred the steaks to a shallow pan and disappeared inside, murmuring something about "letting them bleed in the oven," Sam cringed.

Bogie rubbed his hands together. "Anyone for a game of catch?" He produced a battered baseball from his jacket pocket and threw it to Heather.

"Where'd they make this?" Heather tossed it back. "In the back room at TG&Y?"

81

Bogie smiled. "It's lost most of its zap all right. But I wouldn't want anyone getting hurt playing with the real thing."

Murray leaned against the table. "Imagine, Treadwill's finest playing with a dead ball."

Bogie ignored him and threw the ball back to Heather, who caught it with ease and threw it to Sam. Sam dropped it. "I'm much better at playing the clarinet." She threw it to Bogie, so wide he had to run for it.

Bogie heaved it to Heather, harder this time. Ignoring Sam, Heather drove it back to him, causing him to fall back a pace. "Some arm for a girl." Bogie gave the ball an extra twist. Heather caught it, her feet planted firmly in the grass. This time when she threw, Bogie all but fumbled the ball. He dug his toes in, eyes gone bleak. "Watch this one."

The ball zinged towards Heather, high. She leaped swiftly to one side and caught it. "Pretty good for a ball that's lost its zap."

"Here!" Murray called. "Over here!"

Heather threw. Murray reached up with one hand and plucked it out of the air. He tossed it to Sam, who for once was able to catch it. She was uncertain what to do. What had started as a twosome had turned into a threesome and now a foursome. She tossed the ball to Bogie.

"Over here!" Murray called again.

Bogie blinked, then threw an underhand mush ball. Murray caught it and threw it back. The speed caught Bogie by surprise. He wound up and let fly with a spinner, straight at Murray's head. Murray dodged, lurching awkwardly.

"Nice arm for a jerk," Heather hissed, and everything went quiet.

Sam's father was standing behind her with the steaks. "Would you mind getting the rolls from the oven, Heather?"

Sam peeled foil from the potatoes, conscious of her father's disapproval. "Sit down, everybody, please."

Her father stood at the head of the table and bowed his head. "Thank you for this food, Father. Help us to love one another. Amen."

Murray's head was bowed. Heather's face was wistful, eyes open, staring at Sam's father. Bogie was shifting uncomfortably. "Amen," Sam echoed.

Sam had to admit that her father had been right about the menu. The steaks were just right, and so was the salad. What was not right was the party. Even her father seemed to have lost his usual zest. For the first time in her life, she wished he would tell one of his corny jokes. They were almost finished eating when Sam's father called Heather to the phone. She came back, face gone white. "Excuse me, please. I have to go home."

"I'll go with you," Murray said.

"You haven't had your dessert," Heather protested.

Murray swung his legs over the bench with both hands. "I'm going with you."

Heather turned to Sam and her father. "Thank you for everything. Sorry to break things up." Her eyes erased Bogie. "So long, Benson."

Everyone muttered goodbyes.

"Go ahead with dessert," her father said, picking up some plates. "I'll take a rain check."

What was this? Her father *adored* apple crisp. Sam was even more puzzled when she excused herself and went into the kitchen. Her father was standing by the sink, staring into space. "Go entertain your young man, Sam. I'll manage the dishes." He sounded odd, as if he wanted to be alone, wanted time to think. Sam hesitated for a moment, then went outside with two dishes of apple crisp.

Bogie ate in silence. Sam would have given anything to have the right words to say. It was such a beautiful night. Stars were falling all over themselves for a place in the sky. The air was crisp, not yet cold. The one boy in the world she wanted to be with was sitting beside her. Then why was she suddenly so tongue-tied? Why had her father's bubbling enthusiasm turned into such clouded politeness? And what had changed a simple game of catch into a tug of war? Not that that was all. Why had Heather gone home, and why had Murray insisted upon going along?

Stealing a glance at Bogie, Sam thought he looked as if he wished he were anywhere but where he was. Sam wished he were, too. She should never have asked him. And once she had, she shouldn't have let her father turn it into a party.

Bogie leaned close, his voice a whisper. "How's the beast of the manor?"

"El Loro?" Sam cleared her throat. "He's fine. He likes it here."

"Don't spoil him too much, Sammie Lou. He's got to go back to Fairview once the game's over." He rose with an elaborate yawn. "I ate too much. Think I'll sack out early for a change."

Sam stared past his head. "I'm sorry it was such a dead party."

"It was great. Tell your old man he really knows how to burn a steak." Bogie laughed feebly at his own joke and kissed her, one eye on the back door. "See you tomorrow, Sammie Lou." And he was gone, whistling his way through the back gate.

Sam began putting dishes onto a tray. Her father was

hunched over the phone, silhouetted in the light from his study window. Something told her to wait until he was through talking. Sam didn't want to go inside. All she wanted to do was sit out there and wish she could begin the whole evening all over again.

Her father came out, pulling on a jacket. "I'll be gone for a while, honey." He seemed startled. "Where's Bogie?"

"He went home. He ate too much."

"Oh." He hesitated, then made an attempt at humor. "Tell you what, Sam. You may do the dishes after all. How's that for a case of the bummers?"

He went out the side gate.

Everyone had gone out the side gate. No one had told her why they were going except Bogie. And somehow Sam didn't truly believe *he* was going home. It was only eight o'clock. Eight o'clock of the worst evening of her life.

Sam went inside and put dishes into the dishwasher.

17

Heather wasn't at school the next day. Sam called the minute Bogie brought her home and was surprised to hear Heather on the first ring, her voice tense and wobbly. "What's wrong?" Sam asked, worried now. "Why did you have to go home last night? And why weren't you in school today?"

"My mother's gone. I have trouble getting up in the morning."

Sam bit her tongue. Mrs. Grayson hadn't gotten up to see Heather off to school since junior high. "Why don't you come and stay with me?" Getting no answer, she asked, "How long will she be gone?"

"I don't know. I just want to be here when she gets back."

Sam hesitated, unsure of her ground. If only Heather didn't sound so closed up and strange. "Well, you can't stay out of school forever waiting for her. Please tell me what's wrong, Heather. *Please.*"

Heather's voice rose. "Look, Sam, I don't want to talk about it. So buzz off. Okay?"

Sam reeled with the unexpected attack. "I'm coming over there."

"You stay right where you are!" Heather was crying. "If you come—I won't let you in!"

Sam was still groping for words when the line went dead. She sat staring at the phone, unable to believe Heather Grayson had hung up on her. The hum of the refrigerator suddenly stopped. The house was unnaturally still. Outside, not a riffle of air stirred the shrubbery. It was as if the world had stopped turning, midwhirl.

Sam placed the phone on its cradle and looked at the clock. She had to talk to someone, find out what was happening. Before she knew what she was doing, she had flown out the back and knocked on the Howells' back-door screen. "Murray?" Sam waited with a terrible ache. Would he never come?

When he did, his smile faded. "My mother's practicing her Bach. Shall we sit in your porch swing?"

Halfway across the yard, Sam shivered. "You'll need a

jacket or something. Come on through the back door—I'll find you something."

Once settled in the swing, looking lost in one of her father's camping jackets, Murray asked, "Now, what is it?"

"Heather!" Sam gulped. "She won't talk to me. She sounds—funny. Oh, Murray, what's wrong?"

His long tapered fingers slid up and down the chains. "I can't tell you. I'm sorry, Samantha."

"Does my father know?"

"Yes."

"Why does everybody know but me?"

"*Everybody* doesn't."

Sam gave the swing a sudden thrust, sending Murray's crutches flying to the floor. "If she isn't in school tomorrow, I'm going over there. I'll make her tell me!"

"You can't make people confide in you. They have to want to."

"She'll want to," Sam said angrily. "I'm her best friend. What are best friends for?"

Murray steadied the swing. "I think it is going to snow."

"How much longer is Heather going to stay out of school? Where's her mother?"

"It almost always snows when the clouds look that way." He pointed with a retrieved crutch. "See those white banks off to the north?"

Sam leaped to her feet. "You make me sick."

"That has been one of my keener observations of late."

Sam left him, slamming the door behind her.

She was starting supper when she heard his rapping on the back door. "Well?"

"Your father's jacket." He handed it to her. "And the evening paper."

She took them, the paper still folded. "Thank you," she huffed.

"I'm sorry I couldn't help you, Samantha."

"Ho, ho."

He swung off the porch without looking back. Sam watched him go. He was right, it was going to snow. If it snowed for the big game everything would be ruined. Why did everything have to go wrong all at once?

The phone rang. Sam raced to answer, thinking it might be Heather. "Oh, hi!" she said to Bogie, fumbling with surprise.

"Things are piling up. Do you suppose we could go over to Everett's Pond tomorrow after school? Take the rowboat out before everything ices over?"

"But you have football practice—"

"It'll be short. Gilmore says everyone's too uptight."

Sam hesitated. Bogie was asking her, and not too long ago she would have gone to the moon with him. She sighed, tired of being pulled in every direction. "I'm sorry, Bogie, but Everett's Pond is off limits. Besides, I want to see Heather. She wasn't in school today."

"No fooling." He seemed about to elaborate, then said, "It's okay. I didn't think your old man would let you out of the ivory tower." With a click, he was gone.

Sam went into the kitchen and started some chipped beef gravy. It would probably stick to the bottom of the pan. Chipped beef gravy always stuck to the bottom. She considered biscuits, and settled in favor of toast. "I'm going to quit while I'm losing," she told the frying pan.

She picked up the paper, not really interested. Her mother and father devoured it every day—her father even sent it to California for her mother to read—but to Sam it was strictly a bore. Mr. and Mrs. Edgar Yawn and their three children, Skip, Bunny, and Grace, have just returned from a two-week visit with her parents, Mr. and Mrs. Walleye of Wipeout, Texas.

The headline reached out as if each letter had been released from its own jack-in-the-box.

LOCAL WOMAN ATTEMPTS SUICIDE
IN DRUG OVERDOSE

Sam's eyes blurred. It couldn't be. Not Heather's mother, taken away in an ambulance, near death. Heather's mother drank and took pills. But suicide? Sam read on, "Mrs. Grayson was found by a friend, Mr. Gary Vaniman, when there was no answer to his repeated phone calls on Sunday evening. Mrs. Grayson is the mother of a daughter, Heather, who was away at the time."

How could Heather have been there? She was at Sam's house. And when they'd called her, all she'd said was, "I have to go home."

Sam wasn't aware that her father had come home until she felt his hand on her shoulder. "Oh, Daddy."

"I was hoping they could keep it out of the paper."

"She didn't tell me," Sam said. "I called. I asked what was wrong. She—she told me—she told me to—buzz off."

"Heather is a very mixed-up girl right now, Sam."

Mixed-up? Heather? Why, Heather was the most put-together person Sam knew, tell-the-truth Heather Grayson. The girl with the throwaway humor, making fun of herself, laughing her horse laugh. Why couldn't people be what they seemed? Why did they have to go around pretending?

"I didn't know." Sam hid her face in her father's sweater. "She never told me how bad things were."

"Just wait. Give her time, honey."

Sam sniffed. "The gravy's burning."

Sam watched him wrench the skillet off the fire and set it in the sink—with cold water running around it. Wasn't that a laugh and a half? He knew just what to do, and he wasn't a cook, he was a math teacher. How did people get to know things without being taught? How did they know what was going on in other people's heads when no one had *told* them?

Her father stirred the gravy. "Not a total disaster. Just stuck to the bottom a little."

"Chipped beef gravy always sticks to the bottom."

Sam began making toast, her mind unaware of what her hands were doing. Was it her fault Heather hadn't confided in her? She tried to remember if there was something Heather had said or done that she'd missed. There *must* have been. She just hadn't been alert enough. It was like reading a mystery novel and finding at the end that she had ignored all of the clues the author had planted along the way.

Sam looked at her father over a plate of soggy toast. "What will happen to Heather if—if her mother dies?"

He studied a raised fork as though it might reveal the answer. "I don't know. Heather may be down, but she'll get up."

"How do you know?"

"You get so you can tell the strong ones from the weak when you've taught school as long as I have." He passed a weary hand over his eyes. "Heather's a survivor."

Sam shivered. *Survivor.* It wasn't a role in a school play. It was real. Heather couldn't drop out if the part was not right or she couldn't remember her lines. And there was no looking ahead to the ending—no rehearsing. Heather had to go on stage cold.

As soon as the dishes were done, Sam excused herself and went to her room. Flopping on the bed, she tried to make her mind go blank. Instead, it swirled with questions. What was Heather thinking— What was she doing? Was she at the hospital? Who was with her? Murray? How would it feel to see headlines in the local paper reporting that your mother had tried to kill herself? Sam thought of her own mother and shuddered.

Turning onto her stomach, she remembered Bogie's call. The paper had been out then. Had he known about Heather's mother? If so, then why hadn't he said anything to her? And Murray. Murray could have confided in her, even if Heather had made him promise not to.

Even her father had known.

Sam felt exposed and bleeding, like a cut thumb. Why didn't anybody ever tell her anything?

18

Sam all but ran to meet Murray at the gate the next morning. "Why didn't you tell me? Why did you let me read it in the paper?"

"I didn't know it was in the paper. And I promised Heather."

"But Heather and I are best friends!" Sam wailed. "If it had been me, she'd have been the first person I'd have talked to!"

"But it wasn't you." Murray swung onto the sidewalk.

Sam hurried to catch up with him. "Go ahead. Say it. *You* were the one who saw she needed help—that she was

having problems at home. *You* were all seeing, all understanding—"

Murray neither stopped nor slowed his pace. "Different
people see things in different ways—"

"And *I* didn't see anything." Sam felt a storm of relief,
venting her anger on Murray. "They have ears and they
hear not, they have eyes and they see not—isn't that what
you're saying? That I was deaf, dumb, and blind?"

Murray plodded on, not answering.

"What was I supposed to do when she said she had to go
home? Leave Bogie all alone out there in the backyard? He
was my *guest!*"

Murray stopped at the corner, his back turned to the
wind.

"Besides, I called her! I pleaded with her to tell me what
was the matter, and she told me to leave her alone." Sam
watched the approaching bus as if her eyes weren't focusing properly. "She said if I came over she wouldn't let me
in!"

Murray lowered his head as if studying each crack in the
sidewalk.

A blinding fury overtook Sam. "Well, you can have her
and welcome! Maybe you can manage to stop meddling in
my life now that you're *Heather's* keeper!"

Murray seemed to choke on his temper, turning to
throw his words with deadly aim. "Get yourself another
whipping boy, Samantha. I'm sick of you."

Sam quailed, mouth gone dry. The bus door flew open.
She stumbled up the steps and sat, stricken, her eyes fixed
on the dirty window. Although the bus was warm, her
shoulder blades drew together as if in a draft. A strange silence pervaded the air. Morbid curiosity, almost tangible,
made Sam half sick to her stomach. Everyone's attention
was riveted on the next stop. Heather Grayson's stop.

But surely Heather wouldn't catch the bus today? Not after those headlines, not with all of the students waiting and watching? Through a kind of blur, Sam saw that Murray had taken a seat directly behind the driver, leaving the window seat empty. Sam closed her eyes. The bus stopped. Its creaking door opened and shut, pulling cold air inside, then started moving again.

When Sam opened her eyes, heads were turned like flowers seeking the sun. Heather was sitting by Murray, her back straight, an almost defiant tilt to her head. When Murray leaned to speak to her, she gave out a horse laugh. Sam tried to swallow but her throat was closed. For the first time in her life there were tears in her chest and mouth, but none came from her eyes.

She went up and stood by them. "May I sit down, please?"

Heather looked at her with eyes gone round. Murray waited as if holding his breath. It seemed to Sam that she stood there for an eternity, the oppressive silence crowding her back. Then she saw Heather's mouth turning up at the corners. "Move over, Murray?"

Murray slid, but not towards Heather. "I'll find a seat in back." As he walked the aisle, his low whistle kept time with the scrape of his crutches on the floor. And suddenly the bus was filled with scattered coughs and clearing throats. The students relaxed in small bursts of conversation. The driver shoved his cap back on his head and picked up speed.

The drama was over.

"I'm sorry about your mother," Sam said. "How is she?"

"In a coma. But they think she'll be all right."

"Ha-have you seen her?"

Heather breathed from a place far down. "I've seen her."

"Will you be going to the hospital after school today? I mean, may I go with you?"

"I don't recommend it."

"I *want* to go with you."

Heather stared out the window. "It's just— Well—she doesn't look— I—"

"I want to, Heather. Please?"

They sat in silence, then Heather said, "I told them Murray was my brother. They said only family—"

"You can tell them I'm your sister."

Sam thought about Heather's family. From the time they had been in kindergarten, Heather's family had consisted of her mother, and three "daddies" who came and went. Mostly went. Sam realized with a pang that she had taken it for granted, hadn't thought of it in years.

She vaguely remembered that Heather's maternal grandparents had died in an air crash a long time ago. Few people mentioned it anymore, and when they did their views differed. Some said it was a blessing, since their daughter was breaking their hearts with her wild ways and divorces. Others said it was a tragedy because it had left Heather with no one to give her the security she needed.

Heather leaned her face against the windowpane. "They let your father in. He told them who he was, and since I didn't have a—a father—"

Sam had never seen Heather's father. From all she could remember, he had left when Heather was three years old. People said that Mrs. Grayson had never gotten over it. They also said that Heather looked like him. What would he think if he were here now? What would he do? And what would he think of Heather? What would Heather think of *him*?

"She'll get well," Sam whispered.

Heather didn't move. "She has to."

When the bus stopped, Heather waited for Murray. "Sam's going to the hospital with me, so you can work on the paper after all. But thanks, Murray."

"That's all right. What are best friends for?"

Something raw and biting struck Sam's throat. "I'm sorry I was such a pig."

"Pity. Just when you were growing such a beautiful snout." His eyes rolled backwards like blue marbles. "That trim white knight by the tree is going to break your trim white neck if you stand here talking another second."

Sam ran to meet Bogie. He grabbed her books and stalked off, leaving her to tag along. "Hey—"

"It's almost time for the bell," he growled.

"I'm sorry. But you know about Heather's mother—and I—I mean, she's in a coma. I'm going over to the hospital with Heather this afternoon."

Bogie gave her a baleful look. "Too bad she didn't finish the job while she was at it."

"How can you *say* such a thing?"

"Everyone knows she's a lush. Heather would be better off without her."

"Bogie!" Sam gasped. "She's Heather's *mother*!"

"Some mother."

Sam stiffened as she exchanged her books for others inside the locker. "I'll be late for class."

Bogie held the locker open, hemming her in in his take-charge way. "Your eyes are turning green."

Sam was torn between anger that flooded her brain and tiny hammers that belted her heart. "Sometimes I think you deliberately *try* to make me mad."

"Sometimes I think you deliberately want me to kiss you."

Just as Sam thought he might, he closed the door with one flowing motion. "Good morning, sir."

95

After Mr. Hampshire had ambled past, Bogie slumped. "Wow. All the Beanstalk has to do is flunk me in biology and I'm dead."

"Mr. Hampshire wouldn't flunk you in biology for kissing a girl in the corridors; he'd flunk you if you didn't do well in biology." Yet Sam couldn't help giggling. Had Mr. Hampshire ever been caught kissing a girl in a school corridor? The thought convulsed her. It was as incongruous as Miss Eaglethorpe being caught making out in the parking lot.

"What's so funny?"

"Nothing." Sam sobered. It could have been her father passing by instead of the Beanstalk. The thought brought a flush to Sam's cheeks. Only girls like Lucy Adams carried on that way with boys. She realized Bogie was asking if she wanted to have lunch with him, and said, "I think I'll eat with Heather in the cafeteria."

He moaned. "After school, then?"

"But I told you— I'm going to the hospital with Heather."

"Regular little angel of mercy today." He glowered. "Just to make sure, though: You *are* going out with me after the big game? And I *am* invited to the Backwards Dance?"

Sam's cheeks colored. "You know that."

"Just checking." He stalked off in the familiar slouch.

Sam watched him go with mixed feelings. It was one thing to feel sorry for Heather, to want to be with her and do what she could to help. But it was something else to lose points with Bogie Benson. Points with Bogie were hard to come by. He didn't scatter them around like daisies, even Heather would have to admit that.

I'm going to have to watch it, Sam told herself.

19

It dawned on Sam as she walked down the antiseptic green corridor with Heather that she had not been in a hospital since she had her tonsils out when she was seven. It was a fuzzy memory at best, of malted milks and a doctor who smiled a lot and called her Mrs. Sam. As they passed the nurses' station, a woman in crisp white looked up.

"My mother, Mrs. Grayson. Room 345." Heather swallowed. "How is she?"

"Doing as well as can be expected." The nurse's eyes rested on Sam as a light flickered on a board behind her. "Ten minutes." She hurried off in the opposite direction.

Sam's mind churned as she followed Heather. Doing as well as can be expected. What did the nurse mean by that? Doing as well as can be expected if you've swallowed a whole bottle of sleeping pills? How well was well? Did they say that to everybody? Doing as well as can be expected for a man who's been run over by a truck?

As Heather stopped at a half-open door towards the end of the corridor, something caved in in Sam's stomach. What was she doing here? She didn't want to see Mrs. Grayson, she wanted to go home. Thank heaven it was a private room. Heather walked to the bed and stood quietly. Sam followed.

The figure on the bed didn't resemble Heather's mother at all. The once carefully sprayed hair was straight and damp, held back with a single rubber band. The face without its customary false lashes and rouged cheekbones was now pale and chalky. There was a greenish tinge to the waxlike eyelids. Someone had removed the false pearl fingernails, leaving stubby fingers that didn't belong to Heather's mother. But then, neither did the hands themselves, so limp against the whiteness of the sheets.

Without turning, Heather whispered, "She can't hear me, but I—"

"I hear you." The voice seemed to come from between layers of cotton. "Heather?"

Heather leaned close, lifting one of the rubbery hands. "Mother? Mother?"

Mrs. Grayson's eyelids dragged slowly upward. "So it's true." Each word was thicker than the last. "They said I was alive, but I didn't believe them."

"Don't try to talk. Just rest. I'm here."

"Not—not your—fault— Everything—" Mrs. Grayson's sigh was like ribbon being pulled through glass. "I wanted—"

"Oh, Mother, if only I—"

"Don't cry."

After a silence, Heather said, "She's gone back to sleep. What time is it?"

The familiar dial of Sam's watch was comforting. "We have six minutes."

Heather laid her head on the pillow, still holding her mother's hand. "Everything will be all right," she crooned over and over, until it was time to go.

They left silently, Heather slapping at tears with the back of a hand. "Wait a sec?" She stopped at a pay phone, and after fumbling for a coin, dialed, and waited. "This is Heather Grayson. May I speak to Dr. Humboldt?"

After a minute, "Dr. Humboldt? This is Heather. My mother was awake just now. She talked to me. Will you please tell the nurses I can stay longer with her from now on? Will you do that, please?" Another wait. "I know. I won't upset her, and I won't take anyone with me. I just want to sit with her." She paused, her voice almost a whisper. "She needs me."

Hanging up, she turned to Sam with a replica of her old smile. "He's all right, that guy."

Sam pushed the elevator button. Riding down, she stood on one side and Heather on the other. Two elderly women gripped the hand rails, their eyes fixed on the row of lights above the door. When they reached the first floor, one of them asked, "Is this the lobby?" Sam answered yes and waited for them to get off. She followed Heather silently through the lobby and onto the street, where they waited for a crosstown bus. It was crowded and noisy, making conversation impossible. They got off and walked to Heather's.

"You want to come in for some hot chocolate?"

"I thought you kicked the habit."

"It kicked me back."

Sitting at the familiar breakfast bar, Sam wondered if she would be able to say anything at all, let alone the right thing. The smell of the hospital was still in her nostrils, the sight of Mrs. Grayson's waxlike face still etched on her eyeballs. "Listen," she began.

"I'm sorry I didn't tell you," Heather blurted.

"I don't blame you." Words poured out in a flood of relief. "You must—"

"I thought you were gross. All you talked about was

99

Bogie. All you thought about was Bogie. I even hated you for a while."

"Tell the truth," Sam said shakily. "You couldn't hate a pig like me."

And suddenly it was all right.

"The thing is," Heather said without preamble, "my mother was getting worse and worse. It was bad enough when she had the husbands, but after the last one, well, I think she got scared. You remember the night she came home drunk? We'd had a talk before you came that evening. She knew she was drinking too much, and taking pills to feel better. She knew she had to do something before she ended up in a psycho ward." The electric clock hummed. "And I'd be all alone. She said even a rotten mother like her didn't want her daughter to be alone."

Sam watched a shiny scum appear on her chocolate and lifted it with a spoon. Not knowing what to do with it, she stirred it back into the cup.

"Murray talked to me about Alcoholics Anonymous. The place where people with drinking problems help each other. Mother knew about it, too. She said she was going to a meeting that night." Heather stroked hair out of her eyes. "I was so happy, Sam. We just hugged each other and cried. But I was so *nervous*. That's why I asked you to come over and study—"

"But she—"

"She stopped at the drugstore for some aspirin. Gary Vaniman was there. He said it—the meeting—was a damn fool thing to do, and what my mother needed was a good stiff drink." Heather looked down at her hands. "After you left, we yelled at each other until she fell down and couldn't get up. It scared me so bad, but all she'd done was pass out. I undressed her and got her to bed."

100

"Oh, Heather—"

"That's when I pulled that gin binge. After that, I didn't know *what* to do— I was right back where I'd started. Then Murray told me about Alateens. They help kids whose parents are alcoholics. I started going."

"The bus rides— The meetings—"

Heather gave a rueful smile. "Only I was as bad as my mother. I stopped going. I just couldn't seem to get things right in my head. Mother drinking more than ever, Gary hanging around all the time, and me going to meetings where kids told me how bad things were at *their* houses. Then I went to see Miss Eaglethorpe, and things got better. At least for me, if not my mother." She paused. "If I tell you something, you've got to cross your heart and hope to die."

"Cross my heart."

"Miss Eaglethorpe's father was an alcoholic. So she knew how things were."

"What happened to him?"

"He died. Miss Eaglethorpe and her mother said that sometimes people feel rejected and insecure and do dumb things. Gamble away all of their money. Beat their wives or their kids. Eat themselves into oblivion— Drink—"

"But—I never thought of your mother as rejected and insecure— Why she—"

"Miss Eaglethorpe says she rejected *herself*." Heather took a breath. "And they asked me to give Alateens another try. So I did."

"But—how does it make things better? I mean—your mother just tried to—"

"You don't go to Alateens to stop your parents from drinking. You go to learn how to live with it—how to cope." Heather shivered. "I made up my mind that I'd do

101

everything I could to understand and help. Then she tried to kill herself, and I don't know if I can cope with that or not."

Sam leaned across the table. "Your mother didn't do it because of you, Heather. She said so. I heard her. It wasn't your fault."

Heather's voice was muffled. "I don't know. I get to wondering. In spite of everything they tell me— I just don't know if what I'm doing is right." She raised her eyes to Sam's. "I mean— I never was what she wanted me to be. You know. Beautiful. I used to think if only I were little and pretty, like you, maybe things would have been different."

Sam's words choked her. "You don't have to have a pretty face or figure to be beautiful, Heather. Remember?"

They exchanged uneasy smiles. "That reminds me," Heather said. "You were right about Miss Eaglethorpe having a tragic love affair. She was nineteen and filled with false pride. She sent the young man away because of her father."

"That must have been awful."

"It was. She—she said if it hadn't been for her mother, she never would have made it."

"Did—did you ever know your father, Heather?"

"No." Heather paused, then continued as if talking to herself. "I think my mother's still in love with him—always was."

"Is he married?"

"Yes. And he's never gotten in touch with me. I—I don't even know where he is."

"Do you think your mother kept him from seeing or keeping in touch with you?"

"I don't know. She never tells me much of anything."

"I know. But she's not always—well—"

"Sober. Don't be afraid to say it. I say it often. I look in the mirror and say, 'My mother is a drunk.' Then sometimes I can begin to see it from the other side. She's gotten lost, Sam, and I've got to find a way to get her back."

Sam shifted on her stool, fighting tears. "I wish I could help."

"You already have. By going with me today. By letting me talk to you." Heather slackened as if a string had broken in her spine. "They say she's going to live. It's just that—they can't guarantee she won't—"

The words hung unspoken between them.

Do it again.

Sam felt an unbearable sadness. What would it be like to have a mother who wanted to die? And not have a father to talk to? Sam winced. *Or even a best friend?* It pained her to think she had known Heather all these years, and still hadn't known there were two of her. The tell-the-truth Heather with the throwaway humor and horse laugh, and the Heather who was going through a private hell. "Come and eat with us," she said thickly. "My father's making soggy ooglies."

Heather tried for a natural tone. "What are soggie ooglies?"

"Tuna and noodle casserole. You'll hate it."

Heather rinsed their cups. "I like your father so much, I don't mind hating his soggy ooglies."

Sam waited on the porch while Heather got her things. She heard the telephone ring, and after a while Heather came out. "That was Miss Eaglethorpe. I've been invited to stay over with them for a while."

Sam stared in dismay. "But you can stay at our house."

"Thanks, Sam, but it's better if I stay with Miss Eaglethorpe and her mother. I mean, they're—"

They're women. Sam felt a sudden surge of pure longing. If only her mother were home. "Sure—"

"Wait a minute while I pack a bag, will you? Miss Eaglethorpe said she'd pick me up at your house after dinner."

Sam sat on the top step. A moon was trying to break through some snow clouds but it wasn't going to make it. Maybe it needed to wear some foam rubber pads to cushion the blows. Like her best friend, Heather Grayson.

Doing as well as can be expected.

20

By Friday afternoon of the big game, the excitement that had ballooned all day at Treadwill High had reached a kind of collective hysteria. Sam had never seen the corridors so wild, the quad so filled with feverish activity. Students rushed by as if someone had pushed Fast Forward buttons in their backs. Teachers hurried to their cars, glassy-eyed with fatigue. Members of the team slouched in grim-faced huddles, surrounded by worshipful admirers.

Sam stood by her locker, a bundle of chaos. Where, oh, where, was Bogie?

Her father came by carrying the usual assortment of papers. "Glad I caught you. Fairview's really putting on the pressure over getting that parrot back. There's an emergency meeting of the representatives of the two schools. I won't be home for supper."

Sam's throat thickened. "Be sure and eat something."

"I'll get a hot dog at the game."

Watching him disappear around the corner, Sam all but panicked, ready to run after him and pour out the whole story. Then Bogie was turning her around and she tossed hair out of her eyes to say "Hi."

"You'll have to catch the bus. Everything's nixed except rest for the team between now and the Boosters Club dinner—" He brushed a hand across her cheek. "See you after the game and we'll celebrate the biggest victory yet."

"And the winningest quarterback." Sam sprinted for the all-but-empty bus and plopped down beside Heather. "What's happened? You look different."

"I'm going to the game after all." Heather's words tumbled over themselves. "My mother's so much better now, she says it wouldn't be fair to the rest of the band for me to stay out because of her."

"Terrific. Maybe you can even go to the Backwards Dance?"

"I've already told Jerry I can." Heather crossed her eyes. "He'll think I'm crazy— I'm going—I'm not going— I'm going—"

"He knows you've been at the hospital every day—"

Heather stared at a button on her blouse. "I've loved it. It gives me a chance to talk to my mother. You know— captive audience." Hurrying on, she asked, "Have you seen Murray?"

"They've recruited him to take tickets at the Backwards Dance because some dumb girl finally got a guy to say yes when she asked him."

"I didn't know there were any guys left who hadn't been asked."

105

Heather's voice was flat. "That's like saying there are never any *girls* left unasked, when it's the other way around."

It was a new thought. Sam had always been invited to dances. She could have invited any number of boys to this one, and they would have accepted. "Name one guy who hasn't been asked."

"I'd rather name one who's been asked and said no: Pete Jamieson."

"But why? Lots of girls must have asked *him*!"

"Maybe not the right girl." Heather leaped to her feet. "My stop. Pray I can find my thermals. It's going to be cold marching."

Sam imagined Heather stuffing foam rubber into thermal underwear, and smiled. "See you there—"

Sam was rummaging in the cedar closet for her own thermals when her father called from the school. "Is there a letter from your mother?"

"Yes. I'll bring it to the game." Sam swallowed. "How was the meeting?"

"I came out for air." He sounded tired. "Be sure and bring the letter!"

Sam sat on the edge of the bed after he hung up, suddenly weak. Oh, why had they made her father faculty adviser in the El Loro caper? The thought of him working overtime trying to settle the dispute between the two schools before the big game when all the time his own daughter was hiding the parrot in question was worse than a bad dream.

The phone rang and Heather said, "My mother says I can buy a new dress for the dance, and I'm getting my hair done tomorrow. I have to go. Bye."

Sam found the thermals and laid them alongside her hooded jacket and wool pants. While hunting for her fur-lined boots, she heard the doorbell. Flying downstairs, she opened the door to see four boys standing on the porch.

"Yes?"

"Is Sam home? We'd like to speak to him."

"What—what do you want to see Sam for?"

One of the boys seemed to have appointed himself as spokesman. "We're from Fairview High's team—and—uh—someone tipped us off that a Sam lives here and he has our school mascot in his garage. Are you his sister?"

"N-no."

"Would you ask Sam to come out?"

Sam's mind was a scramble. How could they have known where to find El Loro? No one knew besides her and Bogie, except for Heather, and Heather had crossed her heart. "Are you certain you have the right address?"

One of the boys shoved a paper at the spokesman. "Show her, Jeff. 1264 Elmwood Drive. With a studio over the garage."

Jeff elbowed the boy aside and moved closer. "It's the right address all right. Just ask Sam to come out. We're not going to hassle him— We just—"

Sam took a deep breath. "I'm Sam."

Four sets of eyebrows shot upward and four sets of shoulders flew backward.

"Samantha Grant, actually." Sam managed a smile. "And do I look like a girl who would steal a parrot?"

"Hah! How'd you know it was a parrot? We didn't mention any parrot."

"Everyone at Treadwill knows about El Loro. Why don't you just admit you've made a mistake, and I won't tell my father about it. He's a teacher there."

The jocks formed a huddle, broke and straightened their line. "Okay. So you're a girl," Jeff growled. "But this is the place and that's the garage with a studio over it and we want our parrot. Nobody's going to get into trouble if you just let us go up and get him."

Sam watched helplessly as they walked single file towards the garage, but came to life when they began climbing the stairs. "Wait! All right. El Loro's there. But let me get him. He won't make any fuss if I bring him down."

Jeff rolled his eyes at the other jocks. "That'll be the day!"

Sam tried to summon a wisp of dignity as she passed them on the stairs, but her heart was a jumping bean. The day she had dreaded had come. She would be disgraced. Her father would be disappointed and angry. And what about El Loro? How could she let these clods take him away?

"Wait at the bottom of the stairs." She gulped and went inside. El Loro was pacing restlessly, emitting a series of alarmed mutterings.

"Shhh," Sam cooed. "Everything will be all right." The words stuck in her throat. What kind of girl would lie to an innocent parrot? The enormity of what she had done weighed heavily as she carried his cage outside and down the stairs. Because of her, El Loro would be thrown to the wolves. Treadwill High would be the laughingstock of the Conference League.

Jeff reached for the cage only to be driven back by El Loro's relentless beak. As he nursed his fingers, another boy picked up a stick.

"Stop poking at him!" Sam demanded. "*I'll* take him to your car. And if you don't start treating him better when you get him back to that locker room, I'll call the Humane Society!"

"Look who's talking," Jeff scoffed. "If anyone's going to get reported, it's going to be you. *You* stole the beast and hid him all this time." He turned to the other boys with a cocky smile. "What d'you bet she gets expelled?"

To Sam's horror, she began to cry, but at the same time a flag of anger rose inside of her. "I've changed my mind. You—you can't have him!"

"Stow it." Jeff grinned. "We've got you and you know it."

"I admit that. And I'll take him to school Monday and turn him over to the Student Council myself. But I'm not going to let *you* have him."

"Look—I hate leaning on a girl, but—well— Hand him over."

Sam shoved the cage behind her back. "If you—you want him, you're going to have to—have to come and get him."

They hesitated a moment, then advanced slowly.

A voice from behind Sam said, "Come, come, Samantha. Can't you see you are hopelessly outnumbered?"

Sam turned to see Murray leaning on his crutches with an amused smile. "I don't care. They can't have him!"

Murray surveyed the jocks with a sympathetic cluck. "I'm afraid Samantha always was a very stubborn girl."

"You stay out of this, Murray Howell!"

"And stand by while you defend yourself against four such formidable foes? There has to be a more equitable solution."

"Butt out," Jeff barked, and turned to Sam. "Hand over that bird."

Murray smiled. "Hand over the bird, Samantha."

"You traitor! What's gotten *into* you?"

"I said hand over the *bird*, Samantha. Not the cage. The bird."

"Oh. Well, sure." Sam turned to the boys. "I'm afraid my mother wouldn't like it if I let you take her cage."

"Knock it off! You can't pull a thing like that—"

Murray frowned. "Pay attention, gentlemen. We conceded that the parrot belongs to Fairview, which you seem, however monotonously, to represent. But the cage definitely belongs to Mrs. Grant. We can't let you take it without her permission, and she's in Santa Barbara, California."

Jeff moved forward. "We want that bird and we're—"

Murray raised a crutch. "I would advise you to desist. I happen to be adept at crutch fencing—an art learned of necessity but helpful all the same." The crutch made a slow circle at the boy's feet. "Hand them the parrot, Samantha."

Sam opened the cage and lifted El Loro onto her hand. "Hello honey, hello honey," she cooed, and thrust him onto the nearest set of broad shoulders.

El Loro flew in a flapping circle, nipping and gouging. The jocks covered their faces, dodging the fierce beak and swordlike wings. "Call him off! Call him off!"

El Loro gave a squawk of glee and pecked viciously at Jeff's left ear. "Murder the rest, the rest, the *rest!*"

Jeff dropped to his knees, hands covering his head. "Get away from me, you—"

At a signal from Murray, Sam called, "Here, El Loro, honey—come give Sam a kiss."

"Put him back in the cage," Jeff snarled. "We'll bring it back. Who wants your mother's lousy cage?"

"If you want him in the cage, you come put him in it."

"You gone bananas? I wouldn't touch that monster with anything less than a can of Mace."

"If you're afraid of him now, what are you going to do once you get him back to Fairview?"

The jocks straightened their shirts and brushed dust from their jeans. "He's our mascot, and we're not leaving here without him."

Sam turned to Murray. "I told them I'd take him to our Student Council on Monday morning. Isn't that fair?"

"More than fair. The least you gentlemen can do is co-operate."

"She got herself into this!"

"Forget about *her*. Think about the good of the schools. You are loyal sons of Fairview. Surely you can visualize the uproar that would ensue if this little drama were to become common knowledge only hours before the big game?"

"Tell us about it," they sneered.

"My pleasure. Granted your teammates will think of you as clever sleuths for locating El Loro—noble heroes all. But you have to admit you looked pretty silly trying to take him away with you just now."

"Listen, if you think—"

"I do think, gentlemen. I think that the four of you are

scared silly of a bird no bigger than a rabbit, and, as editor of the Treadwill *Echoes*, I would most certainly have to consider the fact newsworthy." Murray nodded over his shoulder. "A nice editorial, don't you agree, Samantha? FAIRVIEW JOCKS INTIMIDATED BY OWN MASCOT."

Jeff circled his ear with a finger. "This dude cracks me up. If he wasn't on crutches, I'd—"

"Do not let my so-called handicap bother you."

"Or mine," Sam squeaked, lowering El Loro from her shoulder to her wrist.

"You haven't heard the last of this. You'll both wish that Monday had never come."

"*You'll* wish Monday had never come if I am forced to resort to printing that editorial," Murray said.

They stood in collective misery.

Murray gave a careless flap of his hand. "Good-bye, gentlemen."

Sam's spine tingled. The hatred of the four jocks seemed to have melded itself into a bullet aimed straight at Murray's back. "Close the gate on your way out," she said, trying to keep her voice calm.

"Damned crip. Hiding behind a girl and a lousy bird."

Murray swung around slowly, his eyes gone aluminum. "Perhaps I haven't made myself clear. What I want you guys to do is butt out of here."

They shuffled across the driveway, followed by the screeching of El Loro. "Murder the rest, the rest, the *rest!*"

Sam managed to hold herself erect until they were gone, then she sagged onto the steps and stroked El Loro's feathers until he was quiet again. She could all but hear the knots in her stomach untying, but was happy to see that Murray's eyes were a clear blue again. Sam hoped she would never again see them go that strange metal color. "Oh, thank you, Murray! You were—"

The corners of his mouth twisted into the familiar wry grin. "I hate to hit a person when they're down, Samantha, but how do you propose to get yourself out of this predicament?" Rewarded with a look of abject misery, he went on. "I thought you'd come to your senses long ago and take El Loro back, but you seem to have a peculiar talent for digging holes in which to bury yourself."

"You! You knew I was hiding El Loro all this time?"

"Come, come, Samantha. Luckily your father was at the airport and my parents were taking in a movie. You and Bogie Benson were about as subtle as a machine gun." Murray allowed himself a satisfied grin. "How long did you intend to keep him?"

"Only until—after the game." Sam stared at the ground. "Bogie was going to sneak him back into their locker room the same way he and Seth Harper sneaked him out."

Murray seemed suddenly tired. "Take him up and give him something to eat. He put up a valiant fight." After a pause, "You didn't do so badly yourself."

"I was scared silly," Sam confessed. "But I knew they had been mistreating El Loro—and I just couldn't let those jerks have him. I—I like him."

"I heartily applaud. I also like him."

"Murray Howell! Have you been visiting El Loro?"

Murray leaned down to the cage. "What do you say, noble creature? Who's in a peck, a peck, a peck of trouble?"

"Sam, Sam, Sam," chanted the parrot.

Murray straightened. "You have two days, Samantha. You can either use them to advantage, or you can screw them up in ten-minute bursts."

Watching him swing briskly across the yard, Sam called, "I had that one coming, Murray."

She shook her head. How could she figure Murray? Knowing about El Loro all this time and not snitching on her. Coming out this afternoon when those four jocks were after her and El Loro.

Would she ever really know Murray Howell?

22

Sam sat with the Pep Band at the bottom of the bleachers, alternately blowing on her fingers and moving them stiffly over the keys of her clarinet. She cheered wildly, her windpower seriously depleted by the scarf wound tightly around her neck, her eyes blurred by the frost of her own breath. Nothing mattered but the game, and winning.

Yet when Bogie's padded and helmeted figure brought her to her feet with a dashing forty-five-yard run, another part of her was still seated on the cold bench asking herself questions. How did those Fairview jocks know where to find El Loro? Had Bogie confided in one of his friends? Why not? Sam had confided in Heather, hadn't she? And what about Murray? He had known about El Loro from the beginning. Strike that. If he hadn't snitched before, why would he now? More than likely it was Seth Harper.

Pandemonium had broken loose in the Treadwill stands, drowning yells from the opposing ranks across the field. The voices converged into one hysterical yowl, shouted to the rhythm of clapping hands. "Bogie! Bogie! Bogie!" The name ricocheted around the stadium, bouncing off the packed tiers of seats and back again.

The force carried Bogie as on the crest of a wave. He ran a few feet to his right, took one step, leaped, hung in the air for a split second, and threw the ball. The crowd sucked in its breath as the long looping pass sailed through the air. *Touchdown!* The din was overwhelming as the horn signaled the end of the first half.

Music blared, muffled against the delirium of the surging crowd. Lights played tick tack toe on the sparkling uniforms of the Marching Band. Sam spotted Heather, stepping high with her snares, the plume of her hat waving above the field like a banner. It brought a lump to Sam's throat. Then, remembering her mother's letter, she hurried to the refreshment stands.

Catching a glimpse of her father in front of the hot dog stand, Sam tried to struggle towards him through a crush of bodies. Stymied, she held the letter over her head to his outstretched hand. Their fingers touched. He tucked his hot dog under an arm and tore at the envelope, squinting to see. Then, miraculously, he was lifting her off her feet.

"She's coming home. Your mother's coming home! Monday night!"

Sam soaked up the words like a sponge. Then her stomach lurched and the sponge became a hard rubber ball. How could she possibly face her mother on Monday night after what was going to happen Monday morning? Her father relinquished his grasp, his hot dog falling between them.

"You've got mustard on your sleeve." Sam remembered to smile.

The second half of the game was all apart and blurry. It was difficult to concentrate, especially with Phyll Morton standing in the front row, her blonde hair dancing wildly around a tam-o'-shanter knitted in school colors—Phyll Morton jumping up and down in fur-lined boots, yelling, "Go, Bogie, go!" in a voice gone hoarse.

Bogie seemed to hear, for suddenly he was leaping like a gazelle, unveiling a special kind of wizardry. The numbers on the back of his jersey glowed as if written in neon lights. Fairview stumbled in its tracks, and the final score was one for the history books. Treadwill 44, Fairview 6.

The stands erupted in a wild frenzy. A mass of human flesh poured past Sam onto the field, tearing at goalposts, tooting horns and blowing whistles. Sam saw Bogie perched on a sea of shoulders, face glistening with sweat, mouth split in a cuckoo grin. The crowd jumped around him like drunken puppets, chanting in ever rising hysteria, "Bogie! Bogie! We love you, Bogie!"

Sam clutched her clarinet with stiffened fingers, unable to move. The tableau on the field, the arm-waving throng and dazzling lights, all seemed unreal. The bleachers were empty when she felt something cold on her face and realized it was snowing again. She hurried to the music building.

Heather was hanging her uniform in a closet, looking surrealistic in a pair of red-and-white striped thermals, her hat pushed back on her head, foam rubber pads bulging half in and half out of a tacky flight bag with Heard's Travel Agency stenciled on its side. Pulling on a pair of woolen slacks, she spotted Sam. "X out everything I ever said about the guy. Bogie Benson's the greatest."

"They say there were scouts all over the place, mapping his every play—and he's only a junior!"

"First a junior, then a senior, then high school all-American. He'll have football scholarships up to his padded shoulders!"

Sam felt lightheaded. "My mother's coming home on Monday!"

"*My* mother's coming home on Monday!"

They hugged each other, Heather's plume rocking dizzily above them.

"Where are you meeting the hero?"

"Here. If he ever gets away from the mob in the locker room."

"Want me to wait with you?"

"Thanks. I need some quiet time." Seeing Heather pull on her jacket and lift the flight bag, Sam put out a hand. "I mean—I have to talk to Bogie alone. But—ask Murray. Tell him it's all right for him to tell you what happened this afternoon."

"Thanks, Sam." Neither of them moved for a second, then Heather disappeared into the darkness outside.

Sam waited on the steps of the music building, her fingers twisting the gold football, her eyes closed. The last time she had waited here it was for Lucy Adams. The night that had started it all, snowballing her toward disaster. If she had it to do over again, she would— What? It was easier to think of what she *should* have done: resisted Bogie's pleas at the School Rock. Refused to accept responsibility for El Loro. If only—

A sudden ecstatic cry in the darkness brought her eyes wide open. Bogie was loping across the quad, dodging snowflakes. The familiar gallop, horse style, brought a smile to Sam's lips. She ran to meet him. He grabbed her, pounded her back, and whirled her around. Their words collided, started over and collided again. They fell apart, laughing.

"You were wonderful," Sam cried, tears spilling over. "Just super, super, super!"

Bogie lifted her high into the air. "Wasn't I, though?" Ballooning his cheeks with air, he let out a joyous war whoop that careened across the quad and bounced over the snow like a skipping stone. Setting out for the car, he sprinted, turned cartwheels, and ran, all in crazy spurts of energy. Sam hurried alongside, carried by the sheer force of his exuberance. She felt tapped by a magic wand that erased all of her doubts and fears and left her floating as free as the snowflakes.

A booth had been saved for Bogie at the Crumbler. Clusters of students surrounded it, slapping his back, thumping his shoulders, drowning him with superlatives. Shouts of praise fell around him like confetti. Waitresses, the manager, even the dishwasher all came to congratulate the conquering hero. Sam basked in reflected glory, satisfied to be the girl by his side.

A university boy shouldered his way through the crowd, held a whispered conversation with Bogie, and disappeared again. Bogie winked. "Foreign agent," he said, hoking it up, "but never fear. I have my secret decoder."

Sam's laughter died as he sucked in his breath, staring upward.

"Where do you go from here?" Phyll Morton asked, hands on her slim hips.

Bogie hefted a paper cup as if trying to calculate how far he could throw it. "Watch me."

"I'll do that." She turned to Sam with a cookie-cutter smile. "You must be very proud of him."

Sam smiled. "Isn't everybody?"

Bogie's voice was toneless. "Let's get out of here."

Sam clung to his hand as a protective shell formed around him, escorting him to the door. Outside the shell, people clawed at him, eager for a touch, a word, a smile. Bogie forged ahead until the door had closed behind them and they were struck by a blast of freezing air.

Sam felt a dizzying relief. Now she would have him to herself. She could scarcely wait to unburden herself. Strapped into the seat beside him, she was surprised to see that it had stopped snowing. Also that Bogie was driving in the opposite direction of the Point. "Where are we going?"

"Let the other clowns cram themselves onto the Point. This quarterback doesn't want any interference."

A quiver started down Sam's spine as he turned onto the dirt road that led to Everett's Pond. In the instant before he doused the lights, she saw the weather-beaten rowboat tugging at its frayed lines, then Bogie's sweater was brushing against her cheek as he reached into the back seat.

"Good old Billy the Hustler," he said, dragging up a six pack of beer. "Always comes through, even if he does exact the usual pound of flesh." There was a hiss of air as he pulled the tab. "Chugalug." He drank until the can was empty, then bent it double with a crunch of his fist. "Want some?"

"No." Things were not going as Sam planned. "Bogie?"

He had opened another beer. "What?"

"They know about El Loro."

The can stopped midway to Bogie's mouth. "*Who?*"

"Fairview." Once started, the words tumbled over themselves. "They sent some boys to my house today. If it hadn't been for Murray, they'd have El Loro by now. I'm taking him to the Student Council Monday morning. We've got to figure out what we're going to tell them."

119

Bogie hitched himself around. "What do you mean? What did Old Hobble do?"

Sam licked her lips. "Murray held them off."

"That'll be the day."

"Well, he did." Sam spread her hands in a helpless gesture. "The important thing is, what are we going to do?"

Bogie took a long pull on his beer and set the can on the dash. He pulled her close to him. "Sammie Lou? Could we maybe keep me out of it? They won't wipe you out the way they would me. Your old man's a teacher."

"My father wouldn't use his influence—" Sam stopped, angry. "*You're* the one who stole El Loro!"

"You don't have to tell *them* that."

"It was bad enough hiding him all this time. I can't lie about—"

"Just tell them you found him on the old school slab." Bogie picked up the beer can and drank. "You felt sorry for him and took him home with you."

"Nobody's going to believe a thing like that! If that was what happened, I'd have notified the principal. At least I'd have told my father."

Bogie crushed the can and opened another. "Don't shoot me down, Sammie Lou. I can go anywhere from here. I'm on top of the Conference League. All I have to do is keep my lousy grades in line." He tucked a strand of Sam's hair behind her ear. "You're an Honor student. Daughter of old True Grit himself. They'll slap you on the wrist and that'll be it."

His fingers toyed with the strand of hair. His lips brushed across her cheek. "Just take that crummy bird to the Council and let *them* settle it."

"But—I don't know what to tell them!"

"Take the Fifth." Bogie giggled. "I refuse to answer on

the grounds it may tend to incriminate me. The all-American cop-out."

"I—I don't want to cop out."

"You're one of the Queens. They're not going to stomp on a Queen."

Sam pressed her lips together. She *would* be protecting him, sort of. Running interference. Blocking the enemy lines. "I—I don't know—"

"They'll have their dumb bird— What more can they want?"

"They're not going to just let me go!"

"So you get a demerit or two."

Sam had never had a demerit in her life. "It doesn't seem right."

Bogie stiffened. "Some victory celebration. Biggest night of my life, and I have to sit here arguing about a stupid parrot."

"But I—" Sam's words were drowned by the roar from the engine. She tumbled against Bogie as the car whirled backwards and then abruptly forward. Tires slipped in the mushy snow as they sped down the lane leading to the main highway. Sam held her breath as Bogie regained control, his foot pushing hard against the accelerator.

Bogie's fingers drummed a grim tatoo on the steering wheel. Without altering his speed or taking his eyes from the road, he flipped the radio dial. Rock music sliced the air. Sam's head swiveled from the snow-covered trees flashing by her window to the quivering needle on the speedometer. A scream rose in her throat and was erased by the high piercing wail of a siren. The headlights of a patrol car shone in the distance, bearing down on them with ever increasing speed.

"Get rid of that booze!"

Sam's fingers connected with three cans of beer dangling from a plastic frame. As she fumbled with her window, a blast of air hit her.

"Give it to me!" With one wild looping arc, Bogie sent the cans sailing out his window and into the trees. Just as suddenly, the window was closed and he had reached for Sam. "Good old passing arm—never fails me."

Sam strained to see through the snow-stippled back window. "He's pulling you over!"

Bogie brought the car to a slippery halt on the side of the road. "Let's have a greenie! Hurry! Gum. Chlorophyll. Try and keep up, okay?"

Sam was incapable of movement. The blare of the music had died with the engine. The siren behind them wound down like a sick baby's cry. The silence was eerie, made even more so by the circling red light that sent psychedelic flashes across their faces. A heavy-coated shadow blocked Bogie's window, motioning for him to roll it down. "See your license, sonny?"

"Yes, sir." Bogie opened his wallet and handed it through the window.

"Take the license out—please."

Bogie fumbled with the plastic holder until he had freed the card. "May I run up the window, sir? It's cold—"

"Leave it down, please." The patrolman flashed his light onto the license, paused, then leaned to peer inside the car. "Bogart Benson?"

The beam raised to Bogie's face. "You been drinking, Bogart?"

"No, sir."

The light shifted. "What's your name, miss?"

"Sam—Samantha Grant."

"You been drinking, Miss Grant?"

Sam shaded her eyes. "No—no, sir—"

The light scoured every corner of the back seat and floor. "You were going pretty fast, Bogart." The patrolman handed the license back through the window. "Take it a little easier from here on, you hear?"

Bogie's vocal cords seemed to uncoil. "Yes, sir. Thank you, sir." As he began rolling the window, the patrolman said, "Nice game, sonny. Glad I traded for the night shift tonight. It was worth it, even with this snow. Not that I'd ever miss a Treadwill-Fairview game."

"Thank you, sir," Bogie repeated, and remained silent until the patrolman had moved back to his car and the taillights had become two pale dots in the distance. "Wow. I thought he'd bust me for sure."

Sam went slack, unable to control the tremors that shook her. "Oh—ooh—"

He tilted her head. "Poor Sammie Lou— scared of the big bad policeman."

"If he'd gotten close enough to smell your breath we'd have been—"

"He smelled my breath all right."

"You mean he let you go when he knew you'd been drinking? A *minor*?"

"You heard what he said about the game. He knew who I was the minute he saw my license. They're all alike. Never did anything in their crummy lives but work and watch the boob tube, so they get their kicks out of kids like me who give them a thrill or two." Bitterness filled his voice. "Just like my old man. Never gave me the time of day until he found out I could throw a ball straight. Been riding on my wave ever since."

There was a brassy taste in Sam's mouth. "Do you realize how close you came to blowing everything? We could both be on police blotters!"

His mouth found hers. "Bogart leads a charmed life—didn't you know that?"

She smiled, still shaken. "You're crazy, you know that?"

"Sure I am. About you." He kissed her again.

The knots in Sam's stomach began to loosen. This was the Bogie she loved, would do anything for. Not the Bogie who went from fire mood to ice. Just when she thought she might melt in his arms, they fell away. The engine fired and music blared. The car spun in a wild U-turn, hurtling Sam against the window. "Hang on, Sammie Lou!"

"What are we going back for?"

"The beer! It must be good and cold by now."

"But it's dark— The snow—"

He flashed his winner's grin. "Rule number one for quarterbacking: Never throw the ball unless you can see where it's going."

Seconds later he stopped, leaped out, and disappeared into the woods. Sam waited, every nerve jumping. What if the patrolman came back? What would she tell him? She rubbed a round hole in the fog of the window on Bogie's side, then laughed when she had thought she'd never laugh again.

Bogie was weaving in and out of the trees, the three cans of beer in their plastic loops tucked under one arm. Side-stepping, he stopped, raised his arm, and threw the cans, then ran forward to make a perfect catch. Sam didn't think she had ever seen anything so beautiful.

Bogie tossed the beer into the back seat and settled behind the wheel, shedding snow. "Wait'll I tell Gilmore I'm my own receiver now."

What could a girl do with such a boy?

In front of her house, she asked, "Hadn't you better hide that beer?"

He reached back and covered it with a blanket. "Come

on. How can you look beautiful for the dance tomorrow night if you keep worrying?" He kissed her and got out, pulling her with him. Before she could get a breath, he was lying flat on the ground, making angel's wings in the snow. "Look. I'm sacrificing myself. If you don't think you can handle things on Monday, I'll give myself up. I'll kneel down before them." He raised up on all fours. "I'll crawl on my hands and knees."

Sam laughed. Bogie got up and took a bow that set her to laughing harder. Then suddenly, he was standing so close she could see the plumes of his breath. "Okay?"

Sam felt warm all over. "I guess I'll be able to handle it."

"That's my Sammie Lou." His lips rested on hers for a fleeting moment.

Then Sam was all alone on the snow-covered walk with only the sound of his departing motor in her ears. She watched until the taillights rounded the corner, then went inside.

The house was dark except for a light in the hall. It really was a laugh and a half. On the one night when Sam couldn't be trusted, her father had gotten around to trusting her.

Sam smiled softly as she went past her parents' bedroom. Her father, once asleep, could not be awakened with a blast from an elephant gun. Not so her mother, who always stirred at the slightest sound on the stairs, rousing to call sleepily, "Is that you, Sam?" She also knew when to go back to sleep and when to get up and sit on the edge of her daughter's bed and listen.

It occurred to Sam, as she closed her door and sat down at the dressing table, what a truly remarkable trait that was in her mother. Picking up a hairbrush, she pulled it listlessly through her hair. How many times had her mother done that *for* her, late at night, standing behind the bench in her faded blue bathrobe, listening as Sam recited the events of the evening?

The blue robe was a family joke. No matter how many beribboned and lacy negligees her father brought home, her mother always clung to the old blue robe most of the time. "I feel good in it" was all she would say.

Her mother *looked* good in it, Sam remembered, staring at the mirror as if to see her mother's reflection. Her own face peered back at her, eyes round and clouded with worry. Instead of brushing her teeth and getting ready for bed, Sam wandered aimlessly around the room, too restless to sit still or sleep.

Perhaps she should map out a strategy for Monday? What to do and not to do. Count and counterpoint, as in a Bach invention. That was it. She would go downstairs and get some cookies and milk—she couldn't remember when she had eaten last—and sit at her desk and prepare her defense.

Still Sam paced and suddenly she knew that it wasn't a strategy for Monday that was needed, or even cookies and milk. It was her mother. A tear slid down her cheek and she wiped it with clumsy fingers. Without so much as washing her face, Sam undressed and crawled into bed, knees pulled up and eyes squeezed tightly shut.

23

Sam was pulled from sleep the next morning by the steady hum of the vacuum cleaner. It was a cheerful sound, and for a half-waking moment she imagined Mrs. Albright playing Follow-the-Leader with the Hoover canister. Three things brought her fully awake: Saturday was not Mrs. Albright's day, there was a whistling obbligato above the hum, and the events of the past twenty-four hours were crashing down on Sam like a Swiss avalanche.

She couldn't remember ever feeling so happy and so miserable. Dickens certainly had something when he wrote about the best of times and the worst of times. If her father had been asked, he would have gone with Shakespeare and Macbeth: "So foul and fair a day I have not seen."

The long awaited Backwards Dance and a date with Bogie Benson.

El Loro and the Student Council, Fairview jocks, Bogie and the policeman.

Sam ran to the telephone without robe or slippers and dialed, letting it ring several times before she remembered Heather was staying with Miss Eaglethorpe now. After a frantic search through the book, she dialed again. A pleasant, elderly voice said that Heather would take the call upstairs.

"Hi," Heather said.

"I think I have run out of cope."

"Tell me about it."

It was a relief to share it with someone, yet when Sam finished she was greeted with silence. "Heather?"

"I'm thinking."

If only Sam bit her fingernails or twisted her hair into balls like other girls did when left hanging on the telephone. All she could do was look out the window, where the snow was already breaking up in grimy mounds.

"Tell the truth," Heather said at last. "Bogie chickened out on you."

It wasn't what Sam wanted to hear. "Put yourself in his place."

"I'm too busy putting myself in yours."

"He could be all-American someday." Goose bumps raised on Sam's arms like miniature Indian tepees. "Do you know anyone who ever even came *close* to making high school all-American?"

"Nobody. I mean, Bogie Benson."

"Forget about Bogie. What am I going to do?"

"Forget about Bogie."

"I can't," Sam sighed. "And even if I could, it wouldn't solve anything. *I* hid El Loro. *I* have to show up at school with him on Monday."

"Slow down. You don't have to show up with him *today*. Make yourself beautiful for the Backwards Dance tonight. Take it one day at a time."

A headache ignited itself behind Sam's eyelids. "Does that philosophy really work, Heather?"

"It's better than brooding."

"I won't brood," Sam promised. "Tell me, how do you like it over there?"

"I love it. I have a room with a slanting roof and four

dormer windows. The bed is so high you have to climb a
ladder to get in, and the mattress is filled with feathers."
Heather giggled. "You don't lie down, you float."

"What are you going to do today?"

"A cut-and-blow at Mr. Shim's. Practice walking in
heels. Visit my mother."

"Heels?"

"Miss Eaglethorpe says if you are tall, you should make
every inch count."

"When the war is over and my thumbs have healed from
being strung from the school flagpole, remind me to get
better acquainted with Miss Eaglethorpe."

"It never hurts to rub up against a little class."

Sam hesitated. "You have a lot of class, Heather."

"Excuse me while I hang up and faint."

"No, honest. And thanks. I needed someone to talk to."

"Forget it. It isn't often I have the opportunity to string
pearls of wisdom around someone's raspberry Jell-O neck
this early in the morning."

Sam was laughing when she hung up, something she
would not have thought possible ten minutes ago. Dressing hurriedly, she went downstairs. "Good morning,
Daddy."

The vacuum cleaner whined to a stop. "So that's what
happened to my old sweat shirt."

"I swiped it from the Goodwill bag."

"Remind me to look there for my favorite fishing hat."
He flapped an arm. "I am cleaning house."

"What happened to bowling? How will the team get
along without you?"

"I want everything shapeship when your mother comes
home."

Sam rolled the sweeper into a corner. "Go bowling. I'll
finish cleaning."

He slumped as if shot, then kissed her hand. "The self-less daughter. A father's ultimate joy."

"I'll get us some breakfast."

"I have already partaken, thanks. And don't fix any lunch for me. I shall eat the customary cardboard pizza."

Sam watched him fish his bowling ball from the hall closet and pull on a jacket that said *Rotary Rooters* on the back. "You are shapeship, Daddy."

He crossed his eyes and left.

Sam ate some cereal and stacked the dishes in the dishwasher before starting to clean. There was at least a year's accumulation of dust on top of the bookcases. "That's okay," she told the absent Mrs. Albright. "Nobody's perfect."

Later, armed with sunflower seeds and a hunk of lettuce, Sam visited El Loro. He picked at the food, staring morosely at her through the wires of his cage, doing none of his usual acrobatics. When she let him out for exercise, he crouched on her shoulder, feathers drooping. Sam nuzzled his beak. "Remember something, will you? Nobody's perfect."

El Loro remained silent except for a sorrowful rattle in his throat.

Sam could scarcely see the stairs for the blur of her eyes. *The condemned man did not eat a hearty meal.*

Back inside, she made a tomato and cheese sandwich and carried it up to her room with a glass of milk. In the next hour, she washed and blow-dried her hair, brushed an imaginary spot from the dress she was wearing, examined her shoes for dust, ate the sandwich, and drank the milk. Buffing her nails, she kept a feverish eye on the telephone.

A boy who had played the kind of football Bogie had last night was entitled to oversleep. Still. He had said he would

130

call. It was three o'clock. Bogie would call at three fifteen. Sam would let the phone ring four times before answering. He would call her Sammie Lou and say he was counting the minutes until tonight. Then he would become very serious and say that he had been thinking things over and he couldn't bear the thought of a girl as nice as her facing the Student Council all alone on Monday.

Sam flopped backward on the bed, so squeezed tight with wishing that the shrill clamor of the phone made her jump. "H-hello."

"I have something to tell you," Bogie said.

"I know—"

"I don't know where to begin." His voice had a curious pitch, as if he had rehearsed every word. "I saw Phyll Morton at the Crumbler last night after I left you. It's like this. She's taking me back."

She's taking me back.

"I'm taking her to the dance tonight. I know I'm a heel for calling you at the last minute, but I—"

I'm taking her to the dance tonight.

"I'm sorry." He took a breath. "I hope you're not mad."

Sam spoke through a veil of gauze. "Yes, I'm mad."

His voice was far away, as if she hadn't spoken. "I can't help it— I—"

Sam hung up. Her throat was clamped shut, her mouth dry. She had an odd feeling that she should be crying. Weren't girls supposed to cry when the boy they loved threw them over for another girl? Especially when it was the second time and the same girl? Her skin began to burn as if bathed in acid, and she felt a desperate need for air.

Racing blindly downstairs, Sam pushed her arms into the sleeves of a jacket and ran into the backyard. Sinking onto a bench, she studied the toes of her boots. They looked like boots she had never seen before. How could she possibly face anyone, ever again? Worse yet, how could she face the fact that Bogie had been using her to make Phyll jealous?

A shadow crossed the boots. "Go away."

"So he actually phoned you," Murray said. "I am impressed."

Sam kept her eyes level with the crossbars of his old wooden crutches. "I don't know what you're talking about."

"Everyone knows what I'm talking about. Phyll Morton and Bogie Benson were playing two-headed man at the Crumbler last night until the lights went out."

"How would you know?"

"I was writing the sports story of the century in one of the back booths."

"I hope you win the Pulitzer Prize." Sam stumbled to her feet and headed for the back door, but by some miracle Murray was blocking it. "Please! Get out of my way!"

"A very touching scene. It was clear that their stormy ship of romance had found its course and was sailing off into a rosy sunset. All that was missing was the keening of violins. But then I don't suppose even Treadwill's finest can have everything."

"Don't lean on me, Murray. I'm warning you!"

"It was very fortuitous, their getting back together again, because they were made for each other. Don't you agree, Samantha?"

Sam's knees buckled, and she straightened.

"At least you commanded some respect this time around. He did you the courtesy of telling you himself."

"If I command so much respect, then why don't you get out of my way so I can go inside?"

132

"Because I do not think you need to be alone at this particular moment."

"*You* don't think!" There was a new bite to Sam's sarcasm. "When are you going to get it through your head that I do not need you standing around in the wings of my life, feeding me lines like some evil prompter?"

"Stow it, Samantha. Just because some lightweight jerk jilts you a couple of times, you don't have to go into the Juliet death bed routine."

"Looks who's talking!" Red dots swam before Sam's eyes. "You've never been jilted once, let alone twice! You've never even had a girl to jilt you! How would *you* know how it feels?"

"Come, come Samantha. Next you'll be telling me I have to play under Toscanini in order to hear the music."

Sam took a step backwards, not realizing her hands had covered her face until she felt him pulling them away. His fingers were incredibly strong. She twisted her head in an effort to avoid his eyes, but with one free hand, he was forcing her chin around.

"Ahh, Samantha."

Sam drew a shuddering breath and wrapped her arms around his waist, head buried in his sweater. "I didn't mean that. Oh, please—please forgive me!"

"It's all right."

They swayed from side to side in a rocking motion, only his crutches keeping them from falling. "I'm so dumb."

"A phenomenon I have often observed." He rested his chin on her hair.

Sam clung to him, listening to his heart thud steadily above the sobs that wracked her body. Gradually they lessened and she could think. The yard seemed unnaturally quiet. Her chest heaved spasmodically, and between hic-

133

coughs, she blew her nose. "What do you think I should do?"

"Go to the dance, of course."

"And have everyone looking at my open wounds?"

"People are too wrapped up in their own wounds to worry about yours."

Sam hiccoughed. "I'll go if—if you'll go with me."

"I have other plans, thank you. I'm taking tickets at the door and pictures for the *Echoes*. That's why I'm practicing with the old crutches. Look, Ma. No hands."

"You could do all that and still go with me. Has some girl asked you?"

"None of your business." Murray swung off across the yard. "You'll no doubt think of a dozen fellows to ask before you're through."

Sam studied the back of his narrow, well-shaped head. She didn't know how she felt for she had never felt this way before. How could words that had hammered and bruised make her feel better? Was it because Murray had goaded her into crying? Whatever he'd done, Sam no longer hurt so much. She took off the football necklace and clamped it in her hand. Her diaphragm was still jumping with spastic regularity when she picked up the phone in her room.

Miss Eagelthorpe said, "Samantha? You sound as if you have a cold."

"Just hoarse from yelling so much at the game." Sam cleared her throat. "Is Heather there?"

"Very much so. At least someone who is filling the house with girlish activity seems to be in residence upstairs. Just a moment, please."

"Miss Eaglethorpe? It's awfully nice of you and your mother to let Heather stay with you."

"It is our pleasure, believe me."

Sam opened her desk drawer and dropped the necklace in, then closed it firmly.

Heather picked up the phone. "Sam? You have to promise not to laugh when you see me tonight."

"I won't be there tonight, but I promise not to laugh."

"My hair is all flipped out and my eyes look funny— What do you mean, you won't be there?"

"Bogie Benson has switched girls again."

"Oooh, that scumball!"

"Calling him names won't help. It's done. I—"

There was an impatient cry. "Oh, why did I think it was a good idea to stop biting my fingernails? How can I *think*?" After a pause, "Okay. You can't take this lying down. You've got to be at that dance tonight."

"You can't go to a Backwards Dance alone." Hiccough. "I've already asked Murray and he turned me down."

"You asked the wrong fella. There is no boy in school I respect more than I do Murray Howell, but if you show up tonight, it's got to be with someone who obviously adores you."

"I seem to have run out of adorers."

"Not really."

"Who?"

"Pete Jamieson."

"But you said he was waiting for the right girl to ask him." Sam stopped short. "Listen—Pete's no dummy— He'd think I was crazy calling him at the last minute—"

"People who are crazy about other people seldom think they are crazy."

"Are you saying Pete is crazy about me?"

"I'm sure of it. You just got through saying he's no dummy. And Lord knows he's all apart when you're

135

around." Heather was losing patience. "Listen. Do you want people to think you're at home bawling your eyes out?"

Sam sighed. "Do you have his number?"

"You do, too, but here it is: 766–1991."

"Thanks." Sam started to hang up. "Tell the truth, Heather. I honestly don't think I could stand being turned down for the third time in one day."

"Call him."

24

"He's not here," Pete's mother said. "I'll have him call you when he comes in. How are you, Sam?"

"I'm fine, Mrs. Jamieson. How are you?"

"Just fine. Has your mother come home yet?"

"She'll be coming Monday night."

"That's lovely."

Sam mumbled something and hung up. In sudden alarm she ran to the bathroom and splashed cold water on her face. What would she say to Pete when he called? What would *he* say?

The phone rang, and Sam took a deep breath before answering.

"Sam?" Pete asked, as if he couldn't believe it was her. "How are you?"

"I'm fine." Sam swallowed. "Strike that. I am not fine. I mean, Bogie Benson was taking me to the dance tonight, but now he's taking Phyllis Morton. I know it's terribly late, but I was wondering if you're free to go with me. If you aren't, or you don't want to go, it's all right. Just say so."

Pete's voice was surprised, but firm. "I'd like very much to go to the dance with you."

"That's nice of you, Pete. Thank you."

"I'll pick you up about eight. I—I've got my father's car. I mean, no delivery car tonight. And—thanks for telling me about Bogie and all, I mean."

"I didn't want you to get any wrong ideas." Sam started over again. "I mean, I didn't want you to think I was beginning anything again. To tell you the truth, Pete, I don't know how I feel right now. I—I hope you understand."

"I do. Listen, Sam, I do."

"Thank you, Pete," Sam whispered, and hung up.

How differently people reacted than she had thought they would. First Murray, now Pete Jamieson. Understanding. How understanding was *she* when other people needed it? The answer was clear and shocking. Samantha Grant was a selfish, self-centered pig. When she had time, when she had everything together again, she would go over her character with a fine-tooth comb.

Right now she had to get ready for the dance, and she *had* to rise to the occasion. The results were surprising, or so her full-length mirror seemed to be trying to tell her. On the worst night of her whole life, with her heart splintered and broken, she had never looked better. Wasn't it a laugh and a half?

Her father smiled as she came down the stairs.

"Bogie should be properly dazzled. I wish your mother could see you."

137

Sam lifted her head. "I'm not going with Bogie. He's—he's taking Phyllis Morton."

A cautious note crept into his voice. "It might be helpful if I knew just who *is* taking you."

"Pete Jamieson." Sam told him everything. "So I called Pete, and—"

"Thanks for telling me—and for telling Pete. That couldn't have been easy." Her father's eyes glistened. "I'm proud of you."

Sam's stomach took a quick dive. Would he still be proud of her on Monday morning? She was glad when the doorbell rang.

"You look very nice," Pete said as he walked her to the car.

"Thank you. You look nice, too, Pete."

"I was sure glad when you called," he said as they danced the first dance. "It was a super surprise."

"It took all of my nerve to pick up the phone."

"Well, I'm sure glad you did," he said. "I'm having a wonderful time."

Sam saw Heather dancing with Jerry Peterson and did a double take. It wasn't the long cream gauze dress in three tiers with a lacy scoop neckline or the face with its unusual trace of blusher and lipstick. It was the rag-doll hair that now curled away from the sides of Heather's face like ocean waves. As Sam stared, Heather winked a feathery eye and spread her fingers behind Jerry's back.

Fingernails!

Sam made an O with her thumb and forefinger, and watched as Tom Hanson tapped Heather on the shoulder and cut in.

"What?" Pete asked.

"I said Tom Hanson has grown a lot this semester."

"He sure has." There was an awkward silence. "Boys get

their main growth in the sophomore year. As a general rule. Generally speaking."

"And girls get theirs in the eighth grade," Sam moaned. "It should be the other way around." And suddenly the tension was dissolved between them and they were laughing.

"Do you remember when we were in the seventh grade dancing class?" he asked. "My head came up to your chin."

"But even you weren't the shrimp Jerry was," Sam giggled. "I used to be in an agony of embarrassment when I had to dance with him. I could stare straight over his head into the eyes of the other girls. And look at him now!"

"It's funny how important things were when we were little kids, isn't it?"

"Yes." Sam sighed. "It's wonderful to be grown up." Spotting a couple across the floor, the valves of her heart seemed to squeeze shut. Bogie and Phyll were dancing in their own private capsule, Bogie's chin resting on her hair, his cheek slightly turned.

Tell the truth, Sam admitted. Phyll's blonde hair looks much better against Bogie's dark red coat than your auburn would. That truth let loose a flood of others. Happiness shone around Bogie like an armor of light. He wasn't fighting the world anymore. Murray was right. Phyll Morton and Bogie Benson were made for each other.

Sam realized Pete was leading her to the refreshment table. "The grapevine has it," he said, waving an arm at two punch bowls, "left end regular. Right end loaded."

Sam chose the left. Sitting down with the cup, she saw Murray swinging across the room on his wooden crutches, a camera and flash dangling from his neck. He looked taller, somehow, in a blue suede coat and white turtleneck sweater. It certainly was a night for double takes.

139

He smiled at them and raised a camera. "Hold it, please."

Sam smiled as someone jostled her arm. Punch flew in all directions as the camera clicked.

Pete cried, "Oh, that's terrible," and reached for a handkerchief to wipe at the spots on her dress.

Sam set her cup aside. "Don't worry, it's washable." She gave him a rueful smile. "Excuse me, please."

She walked through the outer lounge of the deserted girls' room to the nearest washbasin and examined the damage. Most of the spots were near the hemline. Sam began blotting them between layers of damp paper towels, watching them gradually disappear. Splaying the skirt away from her body, she waited for it to dry.

The outer door opened, letting in a flurry of girlish laughter. Sam dropped the skirt and braced herself, but no one appeared. Instead, there was a creaking of couches, and voices whispering in conspiratorial glee. "Come on, Lucy," someone coaxed, "you promised to tell all."

"Phyll would kill me." No one could mistake Lucy Adams' voice, now rising suddenly. "Stop pigging up! It's *my* Coke bottle, you know."

Giggles. "Where'd you get the booze, Lucy?"

"My father's liquor cabinet." The sound of swallowing. "It's easy if you know how. Just pour out what you want from the gin or vodka bottle, and fill the bottle with water."

"Doesn't he know the difference?"

"By the time he's stopped for his usual three martinis on the way home from work, he wouldn't know if the bottle was laced with Shinola." She burped. "Did you know that if there are eight ounces of booze in a Coke bottle, and only four of us, that's two ounces apiece?"

"Not the way you're guzzling."

Lucy's voice blurred. "Did you see Phyll and Bogie out there? 'I, Phyll, take thee, Bogie, to be joined at the hip until death do us part.' "

"While Sam's blood is circulating green."

"Lucy," an impatient voice interrupted, "you promised you'd finish telling us. So someone sicked some of Fairview's toughest apes onto our star quarterback. How'd they know it was *Bogie* who stole El Loro in the first place?"

"Seth Harper. You know what a chicken he is."

"Listen." A voice dripped sarcasm. "Let me tell you about Seth Harper."

"Shut up. Now tell us, Lucy. What *happened?*"

"Well—" Lucy's voice dimmed. "They cornered Bogie in the student parking lot after everyone else had gone, and laid it on him. He had to come up with something quick or they'd have wiped the pavement with him. It was pure genius. He told them they had the wrong man." Lucy was seized with a fit of giggling. "He told them it was Sam Grant. Get it?"

Sam felt a dry prickling at the top of her scalp. She tossed the paper towels into a wall slot and examined her skirt. It was as good as new. There really wasn't anything like permanent press, unless it was a sturdy pair of legs. Sam's carried her, acting solely on their own, out into the lounge and halfway across it until a voice caused her to hesitate.

"Speaking of the devil." While the other three girls played statue, Lucy shoved the Coke bottle towards Sam. "Have a drink, Sam. It might put some color back in your face."

"No, thank you." A pocket of air was expanding in Sam's chest. She reached for the door, only to find Lucy blocking it. "Pardon me?"

141

"Pardon me—no—thank you. I do declare if you aren't the very Sam Grant we were just talking about. Why don't you come down off your high horse and admit you heard every word we said?"

"I don't listen to cheap gossip," Sam said, and saw that Lucy was silently backed by the other three. A hush had fallen over the room and there was something besides gin in the air. Behind Lucy's cherubic smile and watchful manner was a curtain of ugliness. Why didn't someone open the door and come in? Wasn't there one single girl out there who had to go to the bathroom?

A tall girl moved towards Sam, punching a finger near her face. "You heard what we said and don't try to tell us you didn't. And if you tell anybody, you are going to be in a lot more trouble than you're in already."

Sam's heart bonged against her ribs. What would she do if they resorted to a free-for-all? She was not only outnumbered, she was woefully inexperienced when it came to hair pulling, slapping, and eye gouging. She inched backwards. "So I heard what you said. I not only don't listen to cheap gossip, I don't repeat it."

The tall girl turned to the others for support. "Just to make sure she remembers, maybe a little booze would help?" She motioned to Lucy to hand her the bottle while the other girls grabbed Sam's hands. "Maybe we can pour some on that pretty white dress? My, my, the little old schoolteacher's daughter going around smelling like a brewery."

Lucy clutched the bottle to her stomach with both hands. "You want to throw booze, throw your own." She took a pull on the bottle. "Let her go. She's not going to do anything and she knows why. Don't you, Sam?"

Sam managed to look her in the eye. "You tell me."

They were gone. Sam sank onto the nearest couch,

closed her eyes, and began counting to fifteen. The door opened again. She held her breath.

"There you are!" Heather glowed. "Listen—you'll never believe it. Tom Hanson asked me for a date! And I'm going to play tennis with him tomorrow!"

"That's super. Tom Hanson is a very nice guy."

"What's wrong?" Heather sank onto the couch beside her. "Open your eyes!"

Sam's head was light. "Do you believe in sunspots, Heather? I mean, things haven't been going all that well for me lately, and I was wondering if—"

"I just passed Lucy the Bat. Did she say something to upset you?"

"Who—who pays any attention to L-Lucy?"

"I do." Heather looked as grim as she could with her new face. "*Tell* me."

25

Sam focused on Heather's chin. "What would you say if I told you that a girl who is an Honor student, doesn't drink her father's gin or smoke pot, and is still a virgin has turned out to be the most ripped-off girl of the year?"

"Are we speaking of someone I know?"

"Your best friend and my worst enemy."

"Oh. That girl."

Sam's mouth seemed full of Play Doh. "That girl just learned that Bogie Benson put the finger on her for those jocks to save his own neck."

"That weasel!" Heather broke off with an animated expression as three girls opened the door and giggled their way through the lounge to the rest rooms. "Look. This is no place to talk."

"Don't worry. Rule number three from *Mother's Guide for Growing Girls*: Never bare your soul in a beauty shop or a ladies' room." Sam ran a tongue around the rim of her mouth. "Do something for me, please, Heather? Find Pete and tell him I'll be out in a minute? He'll think I'm lost for sure."

Heather nodded, turning with a hand on the doorknob. "Are you all right?"

"It only hurts when I laugh."

Hearing a flurry from the washbasins, Sam hurried to one of the mirrors and pretended a repair of her lipstick.

The girls drifted back. "Having fun?" one of them asked.

"Loads. But someone spilled punch on my dress and—"

"What a bummer." After more murmurs, they left. Bracing herself, Sam followed. Seeing Pete's face light up as he came towards her through the crowd, Sam thought what a dear guy he was, and took his hand. "I'm good as new, see? And I'm sorry I'm late. Girl talk, you know."

His smile widened. "Let's dance and have some boy and girl talk."

Seeing Murray, Sam winked. "A funny thing happened on the way to having my picture taken."

Murray raised his camera. "Good shot. Thanks."

When Pete pulled Sam onto the floor, she looked at Murray over his shoulder. "Sit the next one out with me, please?"

"I could use the rest."

For once Sam knew how he felt. She hadn't been taking pictures or tickets all evening, but there were other ways of becoming tired. Yet Murray was swinging off into the crowd with a vigor all his own, while she was drained.

Sam rested her head on Pete's shoulder. It was nice to dance a slow dance with a boy who didn't hold a girl too tightly just because close dancing was back in style. Who knew when a girl didn't want to talk. Pete's heartbeat sounded steady and reassuring. The kind of heartbeat a girl could fall out of love by, if she had enough time.

Bogie and Phyll danced nearby, barely moving, fingers laced. Sam panicked. What if he looked at her? Should she smile? Look away? Then she found his eyes looking directly into hers and knew the answer. When looking at a boy in a trance, it is not necessary to respond. Sam looked up to find Pete observing her, his face a reflection of her own. How many times had he looked at *her* when she was in a trance? "You are a nice boy, Pete."

His chin brushed her hair. "You are a nice girl, Sam."

They ended the dance near the pair of crash doors where Mr. Hampshire was standing with Miss Eaglethorpe. Not too long ago Sam would have groaned at the prospect of exchanging pleasantries with the Beanstalk and Old Eagle Eye. Now she heard herself saying, "You look good in green, Miss Eaglethorpe."

"Thank you, Samantha."

Pete was focusing his attention on Mr. Hampshire. "When will you be going back to South America, sir?"

"Not soon, I'm afraid. The government has not yet deemed tree toads worthy of very many tax-supported grants."

"I'm sorry, sir."

"So am I."

It was the first time Sam had actually looked at Mr.

Hampshire. His eyes were a rich brown, and his mouth turned up at one corner as if debating whether to smile or not. "My father thinks you are a genius."

"Nonsense," countered Miss Eaglethorpe. "If he were a genius, he would have gotten me a glass of punch long ago."

Pete sprang to attention. "Let me get it, please."

"I need the exercise," Mr. Hampshire said, ambling along.

"What a crowd!" Sam said. Getting no answer, she tried again. "Did you ever see Heather looking as yummy as she does tonight?"

"The fact that *yummy* is in the dictionary doesn't necessarily mean I like it," Miss Eaglethorpe informed her. "However, Heather does look quite yummy tonight."

"It—it was good of you to let her stay with you."

"I believe you told me that once before." A twinkle appeared in Miss Eaglethorpe's eyes. "Although I am sure I shall be accused of resorting to unorthodox methods when it comes to the teaching of *Julius Caesar*. Capturing the student, so to speak."

Sam managed a weak smile.

"And speaking of capturing, have you solved your mystery of the stolen parrot yet, Samantha?"

Caught off guard, Sam could only say, "Oh, that? Well, no." She stopped and began again. "That's not true. I have solved it, and I wish I hadn't."

"I'm sorry to hear that. Is there anything I can do to help?"

What? Take El Loro off Sam's hands and keep *him* along with Heather? Could a parrot be taught *Julius Caesar*? "No, thanks. I can handle it." Sam gulped. "At least I think I can."

There was an uneasy silence. "I see Pete and Mr. Hamp-

146

shire have successfully evaded the loaded end of the punch table." Ignoring Sam's start of surprise, Miss Eaglethorpe continued. "The Beanstalk could probably use a good stiff drink, poor dear. Chaperoning a school dance is not exactly his cup of tea."

The question was out before Sam thought. "Are you going to snitch?"

"I never have."

Sam had the feeling her mouth was permanently open.

"It is my opinion that young people will experiment in various degrees with the forbidden, in whatever form available. At least the punch is diluted with fruit juice." Her face crumpled itself into an uneasy smile. "It was not a comfortable decision. But since they have ruled it impossible for a student to leave a dance once he has come in, I have reasoned that spiked punch, while dangerous and reprehensible, is better than bottles smuggled into the rest rooms or stashed in cars." The gray eyes impaled Sam with myopic intensity. "I have observed—in my capacity as chaperone, of course—that you chose to drink the unloaded, Samantha."

Sam blinked. Was she truly standing here talking to Miss Eaglethorpe about snitching and spiked punch? "I don't drink. I don't do much of anything wrong, Miss Eaglethorpe, and when I do, I usually get caught."

"You make it sound as if doing the right thing is not a virtue."

A note of bitterness crept into Sam's voice. "I once heard about a man in baseball—I don't remember his name—who says nice guys finish last."

"Leo Durocher. And utter hogwash, by the way."

"Then why do the girls who *don't* play by the rules come away with all the marbles?"

"It depends upon the evaluation you put upon marbles."

Was she hinting that Bogie Benson wasn't worth winning? If so, she had to be bananas. It only went to show that Heather could be wrong about Miss Eaglethorpe. Maybe she was "beautiful" and had "class," but what did she know about love? "In case you are interested," Sam told her, "I am extremely tired of being a nice girl."

"I am sorry to hear that."

Sam couldn't stop. "What has being nice ever gotten you, Miss Eaglethorpe?"

With a look that could have meant anything, Miss Eaglethorpe answered, "A considerable amount of beautiful marbles." Then, showing a serene smile for Pete and Mr. Hampshire, she said, "What remarkable timing. Samantha and I are in dire need of something refreshing."

The punch tasted bitter, and Sam wished that words spoken could be taken back, their rudeness erased. She found small comfort in the fact that Miss Eaglethorpe was still smiling as if nothing had happened. When the music began again and couples started drifting back onto the dance floor, Sam thanked Pete for the punch, and said, "Excuse me, please."

"Save the rest of the dances for me?"

"Every *other* one. It wouldn't be fair to monopolize you."

"Monopolize me, monopolize me," he clowned.

Sam found Murray sitting by one of the exits. Without speaking he led her to the recessed area that served as a ticket booth and cloakroom. Once they were settled in chairs, he said, "You seem to be holding up remarkably well."

"As my father would say, I am keensie peach."

"But not as keensie peach as you were a while ago. Why?"

Had he planted a bug in her head that transmitted

148

thought waves? "The girls' room turned out to be a fun thing. I should have carried my switchblade." Under his cool gaze, Sam dropped her pose. "Not only am I the woman scorned, I am the woman double-crossed. And all by the same guy."

"Ahh me. That means, I presume, that the Fairview boys did not find El Loro's hideaway without help. Help which came from our inestimable quarterback, Bogie Benson. The tattletale? Heaven's fallen angel, Lucy Adams."

How did he do it? "She'll deny it."

"As the saying goes, Lucy lies a lot."

"She also drinks her father's gin in the girls' room."

"If she steals his gin often enough, he may notice and pay some attention to her. I hope it won't be too late."

"Good grief! Next thing you'll be feeling sorry for Phyll Morton!"

"Why not? The prize in the Cracker Jack is plastic."

Sam had no intention of locking horns with Murray on the subject of Bogie Benson again. Nor did she want to sit out a dance cluck-clucking over Lucy Adams and Phyll Morton. "At least one neat thing happened. Heather is having the time of her life. Dancing every dance. And Tom Hanson asked her for a date."

"Heather is going to be a knockout. I hope you're prepared."

"What's that supposed to mean?"

"That born beauties usually pick plain girls for their best friends. Less competition."

"That's a horrible thing to say! No one could be happier than I if Heather turns out to be a knockout."

"Of course. What are best friends for?"

Sam hesitated. "Am I a born beauty?"

"It's nice you asked. I would be worried if you hadn't, because girls who are born beauties and know it are even

149

more of a pain in the neck than born beauties who do not know it."

"First I'm a born beauty, then I'm a pain in the neck."

"They usually go hand in hand."

Sam faltered. "That's the first even halfway nice thing you've ever said to me."

"You just haven't been listening."

Sam's eyes met his for an unsettling moment. She had thought Murray would help, and instead he was like everyone else tonight. Unpredictable.

"Murray? What do you think I should do about Bogie?"

"If you think I'm going to fall into *that* trap—"

"What trap?"

"Of giving advice for you to refute."

"I won't refute it." Sam stared at her limp hands. "Please, Murray."

He hoisted himself onto his crutches. "You'll think of something."

Sam felt a flash of her old impatience. "Like telling Bogie he's chicken? That's what you're trying to say, isn't it?"

"Cut it out," Murray said. "You've made a good beginning with the decision to take El Loro to the Student Council on Monday. What you do about Bogie Benson is something you'll have to decide for yourself."

Sam gave her skirt a fling, near tears. "Keensie peach."

Murray was looking over her shoulder. "Here's your date."

Sam went to meet Pete, and as they began dancing she laid a gentle finger on his lips. "Do you mind if we don't talk for a while? I have to think."

"Well, sure. You just go right ahead and think."

It was all very well for Murray to say she would think of something, but *what*? Maybe if she had told him how she'd felt when she found out that Bogie had sent those four jocks after her. Still. She didn't *know* that Bogie had, did she? All she had was Lucy's word for it, and Lucy lied a lot.

Sam took a breath from deep inside. She wouldn't believe it until she heard it from Bogie Benson's lips. As if in answer to her thoughts, the dance ended and she saw Bogie and Phyll sitting in a corner. A lump lodged itself in her throat. "Wait a sec, will you?" she asked Pete, and went over to stand in front of them.

The muscles in Bogie's jaw flickered. "Hiya, Sam."

"Did you tell those Fairview boys where to find El Loro?"

Phyll poked him. "Would you ask her to repeat the question, please?"

Bogie folded his arms across his chest. "Would you repeat the question, please?"

"Did you send those boys to find me?"

"I refuse to answer on the grounds the question is a stupid one."

"And so is the girl who asked it." Phyll giggled.

"All you have to say is yes or no. I won't tell. I just want to know."

Bogie's face went deadpan. "You've got the ball, Sam. Run with it."

Sam turned away because she didn't want him to see her cry. When Pete found her, standing behind a paper palm tree, she wiped at her eyes. "G-goes to show what happens to a g-girl when she starts thinking."

He took her hand and led her back to the dance floor, holding her in his arms as if she might break.

151

26

"Thank you, Pete," Sam said on her doorstep. "I had a lovely time."

"So did I." With abrupt swiftness, his lips brushed hers. "Could we go out again sometime, maybe?"

"If you want to."

"Next Saturday night?"

"All right." Sam paused. "As long as—"

"Sure. Nothing heavy. I understand. You've got to get it all together." He stopped her with a grin. "I'm too young to go steady, anyway."

Sam suppressed a giggle. He seemed undecided whether to kiss her again or not, so she kissed him. "Good night, Pete."

He backed away, bounced down the steps, and whistled all the way to the car. Turning the switch off in the hall, Sam noticed a shaft of light under the kitchen door. She found her father hunched over the breakfast bar, the belt of his bathrobe trailing the floor. "I hope you haven't been sitting up worrying about me."

He rubbed a hand across his face. "One of the hazards of being a father."

Sam sat on a stool beside him. "Pete Jamieson's a nice boy."

"So I have observed. I am glad you have renewed your appreciation of him."

"Nothing serious," Sam said, fighting tears. "What is that stuff you're drinking?"

"Hot chocolate. You want some?"

"No thanks. I'm up to here in Polynesian punch."

He shoved his cup aside. "I'll probably say all the wrong things, but—"

The tears spilled over. "I have to talk about it sometime."

"You can wait until tomorrow if you want."

"I've waited too long already." Sam took a deep breath and as she did so noticed that her father had braced himself. What did he expect to hear? That she was smoking pot? Making out? *In trouble?* "Relax," she told him. "I'm not pregnant or anything."

"Good. I'm much too young to be a grandfather."

It gave Sam courage. "Fairview's mascot is in our studio. I did it for Bogie Benson. Friday afternoon four football players from Fairview came to get El Loro but Murray sent them away. I'm taking the parrot to the Student Council on Monday." Sam watched tears fall onto the countertop. "I—I found out tonight that Bogie had told them where to find El Loro."

Her father emitted a long drawn-out sigh.

"I'm so ashamed. I know you're disappointed in me—and mad."

"You bet I am." He pulled his cup back and took a large gulp of chocolate. "Parents always have the hope their children won't be as adolescent during adolescence as they were. Which only goes to show how adolescent parents can be." He laid a hand over hers. "But I am also proud, Sam. You told me. You're taking the responsibility for El

153

Loro. You went to the dance after Bogie stood you up."

Blood rushed to Sam's face. "I asked him—you know—if he was the one."

"What did he say?"

"Nothing. Phyll Morton was with him so he had to bluff it out."

Her father stirred his chocolate. "Are you planning on telling the Council about his part in this thing?"

"I don't know. I have to sleep on it." Sam longed to change the expression on her father's face. "Bulletin: Heather was the belle of the ball tonight. Isn't that super? And if you dare say one word about every cloud having a sliver lining, I shall be sick." Sam gave a tired giggle. "Even Mr. Hampshire was interesting."

"Next you'll be saying your father is not a cornball."

"Nothing has changed that much." Sam poured more chocolate into his scummy cup. "What did you make this with? Thirty-weight?"

He got up and dumped the chocolate into the sink. "I am going to bed."

"Would you do me a favor, Daddy? Resign from the faculty adviser thing?"

His hands spread in a helpless gesture. "You are getting more like your mother every day—pulling thoughts out of my head with your picky little tongs."

"Promise?"

"Promise."

"And—don't worry. I mean— I'll be all right, Daddy."

He came back to plant a kiss on her forehead.

"Where there's a way there's a will," he said.

27

Sam entered the meeting room shortly before nine on Monday morning. Everyone was there. Her father, Fairview's faculty adviser, Student Council members from both schools, Mr. Coopersmith, coaches and assistant coaches. (Where were the referees?) Murray for the *Echoes*. (Also as a Council member.) A girl with red plastic-rimmed glasses and yellow hair for the *Fairview Fanfare*.

Samantha Grant, the accused.

Her feelings were difficult to analyze. Sam recognized the guilt, the wishing that the floor would open up and swallow her. She accepted the incongruity of her position—on the wrong side of something for the first time in her life—on trial, with nowhere to hide. But there was an added something Sam hadn't counted on that surprised her. Her head was astonishingly clear.

Hello, head. Where were you when I needed you most?

Sam straightened as a rap on the table brought a semblance of order. It was suddenly of the utmost importance that she not forget a single thing about this day, this hour, this minute. As if watching through a window, she saw herself setting the recorder in her head to Start, and tuning the television behind her eyes to "Living Color."

Her father arose. "I would like to submit my resignation

155

as Treadwill's faculty adviser due to a conflict of interest."

Sam blinked back the moisture that clouded her eyes.

Mr. Coopersmith nodded. "May I suggest Miss Eagle-thorpe as an alternate?"

Someone went to fetch Miss Eaglethorpe. Sam pictured the students throwing paper darts at the bust of Shake-speare in her absence. One point for an ear, five for the nose, ten for an eye, and twenty for the iris. Thirty for the pupil, bull's-eye.

Miss Eaglethorpe came in and quietly took a chair, oblivious to the foot shufflings and throat clearings. How could so much dignity and poise be wrapped up in such a plain, drab figure? Sam wished it were possible to smile at her, but she supposed a member of the jury (it *was* a jury, wasn't it?) should not be influenced by the accused.

"Before turning the meeting over to the Councils," Mr. Coopersmith began, "I would like to ask Samantha if there is anything she has to say."

Sam lifted her head. "I want everyone to know that my father knew nothing about my hiding El Loro. That's all."

A member of Fairview's Council rose. "Why did you hide him?"

"Because I was stupid. I take full responsibility for my actions."

"Are you trying to tell us that you—a girl, all alone—kidnapped a parrot from a boys' locker room?"

Sam stared straight ahead. "I hid him."

"But you had to *have* him before you could hide him. Where did you get him?"

"Off our School Rock."

There was a round of titters.

"He was just sitting there on your School Rock and you picked him up and took him home with you?" Getting no

156

answer, he bored in. "How did you manage to do that? El Loro's dislike of people is pretty well known."

"That's because you people—" Sam bit back the words. "He was mean and bad-tempered when I found him, I'll admit, but he was also hysterical and half-starved."

The boy hurried on. "When four members of our team went to your school on a tip from one of your classmates, they were told by a member of your football team where they could find our mascot. Do you still deny that someone helped you hide the parrot? Bogie Benson, for instance— Seth Harper?"

"You'd—you'd have to ask *them* about that."

The Council representatives went into a huddle with Treadwill's representatives. Coaches and assistant coaches went into huddles with coaches and assistant coaches. Mr. Coopersmith conferred with Miss Eaglethorpe, who in turn spoke to Sam's father.

"Would you be so kind, Mr. Grant, as to find Bogart Benson and Seth Harper and bring them back with you?"

A lump formed in Sam's stomach, and she thought, Never send a father to do a daughter's work.

A hush fell on the room as the two boys came in and took seats. Bogie's glance slid around the room as Mr. Coopersmith began to speak.

"We have been discussing the case of Fairview's mascot. He was brought to school this morning by Samantha Grant, who admits that she has been keeping him. In trying to put the pieces of the puzzle together, your names were mentioned. Do either of you have anything to say?"

Bogie's face was smooth. "I have a right to know what's been said about me."

Sam reddened. "I haven't told them anything."

Fairview's representatives set up a flurry of accusations,

157

bringing another rap from the table and an admonition from Mr. Coopersmith. Fairview's spokesman said, "It has been said that you told four members of our team where to find El Loro. Is this true?"

"Sure." Bogie curled his lip. "It was getting to be a bore. Let them have him."

"But how did you know where El Loro was?"

"A little bird told me."

Another Fairview member rose. "According to what we've heard, a Treadwill student informed members of our team that you, Bogie Benson, were the one who stole El Loro. You and Seth Harper. They went to your school and confronted you with this and you told them they had the wrong man."

Bogie sat up, face gone crimson. "Are you going to take their word against mine?"

A strangled sound came from Seth's tortured face. "We did it!" he blurted. "Bogie and me. We took the parrot." He turned to Bogie with a pleading look. "Lucy Adams found out, Bogie. *She* told them. They— they came after me, too. I had to tell, Bogie, honest—"

Bogie half rose, then crumpled. "It was a joke. We never intended to *keep* him. It was her—" He pointed to Sam. "It was her idea to keep him."

"She didn't have anything to do with it until the bird got away from Bogie," Seth prattled. "He talked her into keeping him."

"Order, please. Order, please!" When things had quieted, Mr. Coopersmith said, "Samantha, you may leave the room. Also Bogart and Seth. We will call you when we want you, so don't wander away."

It seemed a mile from Sam's chair to the door, an eternity before her fingers had negotiated the knob. To her immense relief, she found Heather leaning against the wall outside.

Bogie gave Heather a withering look. "Scavenger."

"Stool pigeon."

Bogie stationed himself across the hall, Seth dogging his heels. "Get away from me, you scumball."

"They won't do anything to you," Seth whined. "You're Bogie Benson. Why, they couldn't win a game against a tribe of midgets without that arm of yours."

"You stink."

Heather turned her back on them and asked Sam, "What *happened*?"

"I pleaded guilty by reason of stupidity. Seth spilled everything. Bogie blew it. We're all out for the count."

"Are you telling me they finally nailed old Benson with something?"

Sam studied the octagonal patterns of the tiled floor. "I feel sorry for him."

"So they'll take away his magic football."

"No, honest, I do."

Heather sighed. "Yeah. Bogie ain't much, but he's all he's got."

"I wish it were all over. It's like the Inquisition."

Heather's eyes burned. "They're blowing it all out of proportion. You'd think someone had stolen the stadium."

The door opened and Miss Eaglethorpe beckoned to Sam.

"Say a prayer," Sam whispered.

"Prayer." Heather took up her vigil by the door.

Sam sat down in the meeting room, legs stiff.

"You have the good fortune to have had a character witness in your behalf," the Fairview spokesman said.

"Murray Howell has suggested that El Loro be brought in to corroborate his statements."

A side door opened and Sam's father came in with El Loro in his cage. When he opened the door, the parrot flew straight to Sam's shoulder and rubbed his beak against her cheek.

Sam nuzzled him. "Poor baby."

Miss Eaglethorpe motioned to a Fairview Council member. "Will you please take the parrot from Samantha?"

He stepped reluctantly forward, only to be greeted by a flurry of wings and ferocious squawkings. "Murder the rest, the rest, the *rest!*"

The boy retreated. There was a hurried consultation. Fairview's faculty adviser said, "The point is well made. While we feel that our mascot should not have been stolen and kept so long by members of your student body, it is evident he has been treated well. It is also evident that he does not belong in a boys' locker room. We are willing to discuss recommendations regarding his future."

Miss Eaglethorpe suggested the Humane Society, bringing a cry of anguish from Sam, which in turn brought her father to his feet.

"If it should prove agreeable to all parties concerned, I will take full responsibility for the parrot. You have my word on it."

A vote was taken. Mr. Grant was given full custody of El Loro. Sam breathed a sigh of relief as she put the parrot back in his cage. "Everything's going to be all right."

El Loro cocked his head.

"You can believe me this time."

Her father took the cage and left the room.

Miss Eaglethorpe rose. "It is the judgment of this Council, Samantha, that you be given six demerits and be suspended from school for a period of one week. However, due to your past record of good conduct and high scholastic rating, the suspension has been suspended." Aware of the semantics of her statement, she gave a small smile and went to the door to summon Bogie and Seth.

Bogie shrugged his way to a chair, followed by knuckle-cracking Seth. Fairview's faculty adviser spoke. "Before giving our decision concerning your participation in the unfortunate kidnapping of our parrot, it is my duty to caution you all. The administration of both schools is aware of the tension and excitement that accompanies a game between Fairview and Treadwill. A certain amount of heated rivalry is not only expected, it is often condoned. However, in this case, the welfare of a helpless creature was in jeopardy. Such actions will not be tolerated in the future, by any student, in either school." After a brief pause, he sighed. "Now, as for these two boys."

It was over before Sam had a chance to catch her breath. Bogie was suspended for a week. Both he and Seth were benched for the remainder of the football season. "Thank you all for attending. Meeting dismissed. You may return to your classrooms."

Sam left with Bogie's eyes boring holes in her back.

"No rope burns?" Heather asked expectantly.

"Just on my conscience."

They stood awkwardly for a moment. "I saw your father. He's neat. Imagine taking a parrot to math class with you."

Sam could still smile. "He knows real class when he sees it."

Miss Eaglethorpe hurried past, calling over her shoulder. "Half an hour of English left, girls."

Heather deliberately slowed until Miss Eaglethorpe was out of sight. "Now *tell* me."

"Six demerits and a suspended suspension."

"Whee. Could have been worse. What about the Gold Dust twins?" she asked, and listened to Sam recite the verdicts. "Remainder of the season?" Heather exploded. "What season? There's only one game left and we could beat Hunter High with the Junior Varsity! And Seth Harper. What a farce. If they ever let him off the bench, he'd trip over his hangnails!"

Sam didn't answer. She was filled with a strange detachment.

"Listen, Sam. How do you feel?"

"I don't know. I've never felt this way before." She tried to think what school would be like for a week without Bogie Benson. Not to see him in the corridors, hear his Ford revving up in the parking lot. She must be tireder than she thought, for she couldn't seem to care.

Sam didn't like it. She had cared about Bogie for so long, not caring about him made her feel lost and empty. "I hope being suspended doesn't hurt Bogie's eligibility."

"No way. The only thing that could stop a potential high school all-American at this stage of the game would be a broken leg." Heather emitted her horse laugh. "Not a bad idea."

The door of the English room opened. "How nice of you to trumpet your arrival," Miss Eaglethorpe said.

Heather slid past with a mumbled apology.

Sam gulped. "May I be excused, Miss Eaglethorpe?"

"Aren't you feeling well?"

"That's what I want to find out."

"Proper sentences do not ordinarily end with a preposition."

"I'm sorry. I mean, I've got my head sort of halfway on and I want to go somewhere quiet and see if I can finish the job."

162

"Let me know if it fits." Miss Eaglethorpe closed the door.

Sam turned blindly. "Oops!"

Murray steadied himself with a growl. "You might turn on your blinker signals when you're making a U turn." He leaned against the wall. "Feeling let down?"

"More like run over." Sam ran a hand over her eyes. "It's like the hiccoughs. Once I get started, I can't stop. Ending sentences a preposition with, I mean." She sobered, enveloped in the depth of his eyes. A quiet place. A place where a girl could try on heads until she found one that was the right fit. "You know what?"

"It seems to be your favorite question."

"I'm not on Tilt anymore." Sam was glad he hadn't laughed. Because she was no longer Sam Grant or Samuel Grant's daughter, or Bogie Benson's twice-jilted girlfriend, or the Honor student with the lost head. She was herself. All together. She wanted to grab Murray. Hug him. Seal it in blood. All she could do was smile. "Thank you."

"For what?"

"Being right about the prize in the Cracker Jack." She watched a grin spread across his face, "And for being a character witness for me."

"I did that as much for El Loro as for you. I didn't want those apes at Fairview to have him back."

With sudden weakness, as if drained by a long and difficult journey, Sam laid a hand over her heart. "Friends?"

"Friends."

"Forever?"

"Forever."

After a long moment, Murray dug into his back pocket for a handkerchief and reached to tilt her face. "You seem to have something in your eye." As he wiped the tears away, he leaned and kissed her gently on the forehead, seemingly unaware that Mr. Hampshire was harrumphing his way down the corridor. Handing the handkerchief to Sam, Murray said, "You are late for English."

"I don't have to go," she sniffed. "I'm free."

He consulted his watch. "Want to see how El Loro's doing in math?"

Sam giggled. "Probably getting all A's."

As they neared her father's room, students began pouring into the hall, laughing and talking in an animated fashion. Inside, a group of stragglers crowded around the massive desk. Sam waited with Murray until they had drifted away, then approached her father.

"Has it occurred to you, Mr. Grant, that it could be against the rules to teach with a parrot on your shoulder?"

Her father ran a smooth hand over El Loro's feathers. "Some rules were meant to be broken." He suddenly discovered papers on his desk that needed rearranging. "I hear you were given some demerits."

"Six. Richly deserved."

He looked close into her eyes. "How are you?"

"Keensie peach." She sobered. "I am wounded but I am not slain. I shall lie down and bleed awhile and rise to fight again."

"You may not have that quite right—ask Miss Eaglethorpe—but I applaud." The pride in his voice seemed to reach inside of Sam and squeeze her chest. Then all three of them were laughing while El Loro cocked his head and stared as if they had all gone bananas.

28

"Honestly," Sam told Heather out by the School Rock the next afternoon, "you should have heard my mother. She kept going around patting things, saying, 'Hello, stepstool, hello icebox,' and Daddy kept pulling at her and laughing, and she got all tangled up in his arms and I thought he was going to carry her upstairs. Most of all, she said, 'Everything's the same. Everything's just the same.' "

"That's mellow."

"Everything's mellow."

"How's your grandmother?"

"Doing great. She's really a super person."

"I'd like to meet her. I am seriously short on grandmothers."

A swelling began in Sam's throat. Heather was seriously short on family, period. Unless you could count Miss Eaglethorpe and her mother. How would it feel to be so alone, with a mother who—?

"How are you doing, Heather? I mean, *really*."

"I am really doing okay. Busy teaching myself to walk on a tightrope. If you balance the pole just right and don't lose your nerve, I am told it is quite rewarding." Heather smiled. "My mother and I are going to take things a day at a time and go to our meetings, hoping we can keep what ground we've gained."

"I hope you do."

"I have to learn to stay on the tightrope even if she doesn't make it." Heather shook herself. "But we can talk to each other now, and we never could before. She even talks about my father."

"What about your father? Wouldn't—I mean—don't you ever—?"

"Sure. But no way. If he'd wanted to see me, he'd have done it a long time ago."

They were silent a moment, then Heather gave a replica of her horse laugh. "What about you? Are you planning on telling your mother what happened while she was gone?"

"Someday. Oh, not about El Loro and Bogie and everything. I'll tell her that as soon as she stops talking to the furniture. I mean—well, maybe she thinks everything is just the same, but it's not. I'm—well—"

"Tell the truth. You're not the same."

"No. I even feel sorry for Bogie. He was only doing what I was, and willing to do most anything to make what he wanted come true. We can't make people feel things they don't feel." Sam hugged herself. "I just don't feel the same about anything."

Heather was quiet, staring at her new fingernails. "We've all changed. Nothing's the same."

"Except Murray."

"Murray." Heather nodded. "It's funny—he's the strongest one of all—even with—"

"I know," Sam said quietly, then laughed. "Have you seen his *Echoes* extra?" She pulled a red flyer out of her binder. On it was a line drawing of a parrot in a cage. The balloon over its head said, "Anyone can be a fool. The trick is not to act like one." Down in the corner, a baby parrot sat with an open beak. "I wish I'd said that."

Heather grinned. "Murray will probably win the Pulitzer Prize some day."

"He's already up for a statewide journalism award." Sam shaded her eyes. "Here comes Tom Hanson."

"Excuse me while I faint."

Sam watched them walking across the quad together, then leaned back with her face to the sun and closed her eyes. The sounds from the football field made a kind of pattern, like the different instruments in an orchestra. Almost everything had a pattern if a person listened long enough. Even the sound of crutches swishing through the grass. Sam blinked into a pair of incredibly blue eyes. "Hello. That was a really super extra."

"Glad to hear it. You may now observe while I finish on the paper, and your mother will come and take us home."

A warm glow spread through Samantha. "She's probably out talking to the car this very minute. 'Hello, car. Do you want to pick up Murray and Samantha?' "

"Samantha?"

"It *is* my name."

They looked at each other and smiled, then Murray said, "The crew will be waiting."

Samantha slid down and straightened her skirt. "Presto digitalis," she said.